Practical Guide to Online Safety for Students and Teachers

AF428798

The Online Safety Playbook

Arun Soni

First Published by

An Imprint of BlueRose Publishers

ISBN:

Editor/Typesetter: Mohammad Afzal

Illustrator: Morin Talwar

BLUEROSE PUBLISHERS
www.bluerosepublishers.com
info@bluerosepublishers.com
+91 8882 898 898

Contents

Preface

Cybercrime is increasing at a pace not known before. It is a 'technical pandemic' that has surpassed the actual Covid pandemic we are suffering from right now. The vaccines are 'Cyber safety Awareness' and practising 'Digital Hygiene'. Except for these vaccines, nothing else can help prevent us and our Internet-connected devices from this 'technical pandemic'.

The cause that Cybercrime is rising so much is because people are not aware of the basics of cyber safety. Moreover, they live in an ignorant world where Cybercrime always happens to someone else. But slowly, people are realizing and waking up to the fact that they need awareness to counter Cybercrime. Many countries are taking the initiative to introduce cyber safety in the school curriculum. Everybody, irrespective of age, needs to become wiser and aware by learning the ABC's of Cybersecurity.

There are books, but primarily uninteresting and without any practical activity to perform or assess what one has learnt. Those are just long paragraphs in black ink, printed on white or yellow paper. How can these books generate curiosity and interest in a topic? Considering this, we have come out with a combination of valuable content, characters, practical activities, questions to assess yourself, all woven in a storyline. The interacting characters will make this book attractive for young IT enthusiasts.

The screenshots, trademarks, service marks, trade names, product names and logos appearing on images are property of their respective owner and has been used according to the guidelines. If any copyrighted material has not been acknowledged or used as per guidelines in this publication, we apologize. In that case, please write and let us know to rectify it in any future reprint.

This book is ripe with more than a decade of experience as a cybersecurity trainer and 25 years in writing books on various topics of Information Technology, of the author. Moreover, this book comes with 24×7 support by emailing the author at info@arunsoni.in for any query or guidance.

Foreword

The author is a torchbearer of cybersecurity awareness, not only on the academic front but also on the personal front. It's not an easy task to try and create awareness among well-educated people to understand the good from the bad. The issue around cyberspace has always been intangible aspects, which are not visible, and no one can see what's coming towards them. So, just like ostriches, even human beings think that as long as they keep their eyes shut, they need not fear anything. But, dear friends, the threat is real, and that is what this book is all about.

I can practically never forget the moment when Arun Ji asked me to write the foreword for his book. I went through each page of the book with the same level of excitement. What I could not believe was that someone could explain cybersecurity in such simple words and without intimidating the reader. As for me, I firmly believe in the statement passed by Socrates — *"We know nothing, and we need to keep learning."*

The entire concept of the book is so clear that it must reach the masses and, most notably children, because they have been increasingly becoming victims of cybercrime due to excessive use of the internet and technology. This will also make teachers understand how to explain the concepts and problems of the cyber world to children in the easiest language possible. The pictorial representations give us a visual understanding of the same, and they get embedded in our minds.

I wish that each person who picks up this book gets to learn something important from it. This is a masterpiece of its kind. It is time for cybercriminals to beware as awareness is taking shape.

Divya Dwivedi
Advocate
Supreme Court of India
Member: Supreme Court Bar Association
Member: Bar Council of Delhi
Alumni: The Hague Academy of International Law
Delegate: The Harvard Project for Asian and International Relations (HPAIR 2021)
B.Tech (Information Technology), MBA (International Business),
LLB (IP Laws) (IIT-Kharagpur)
PG Diploma in International Environment Laws (The Indian Society of International Law)
PG Diploma in Cyber Law & Cyber Forensics (pursuing) (NLSIU-Bangalore)
Fellow Fall 2021: Center for AI and Digital Policy
Founder & Director: JND Charitable Trust(www.jndctrust.org)

Cybercrime Types and necessary Precautions

a. Types of Cybercrimes
b. Basic steps to protect yourself on the Internet

What is Cybercrime?

Cybercrime is any criminal activity that involves a computer, networked device or a network. While cybercriminals carry out the majority of Cybercrime to profit, some cybercrime is carried out directly against computers or devices in order to damage or disable them. Others spread viruses, unlawful information, photos, and other items via computers or networks.

Ransomware attacks, email and internet fraud, identity fraud, and attempts to steal financial accounts, credit cards, or other payment card information are all examples of Cybercrime. Cybercriminals may steal and resell an individual's personal information or corporate data. Cybercrime is projected to increase in regularity in 2021 as more people settle into remote work patterns as a result of the epidemic.

The first class of cybersecurity class was going on. All students were listening attentively. The topic was various types of cybercrimes and the basic steps which one can take for cybersafety.

Social Engineering

The base of most of the attacks is Social engineering. So first, we will be learning about Social Engineering.

The term "social engineering" refers to many harmful behaviours carried out through human relationships. It employs psychological manipulation to dupe users into committing security errors or disclosing sensitive information. Most of the malware gets downloaded by clicking on infected email attachments, website links etc. Cybercriminals use their social engineering skills to make you believe that the link is safe, and you can click on it.

Most cybercriminals are great manipulators, but that does not mean they are always technological manipulators. Many cybercriminals prefer the art of human manipulation.

In other words, they prefer social engineering, which means using human faults and habits to launch a cyberattack. Imagine a cybercriminal impersonating an IT specialist and requesting your login details to fix a security problem on your equipment for a simple social engineering example. If you supply the information, you have just handed the wrong individual the credentials to your account, and he didn't have to send you a malicious link or hack into your computer. The fault is of the user's as they did not verify the identity of the cybercriminal.

Phishing

This is a method of obtaining personal information such as credit card numbers and username/password combinations by posing as a reputable business. Email spoofing is a standard method of phishing. You've most likely received emails with links to legitimate-looking websites. You probably thought it was suspicious and did not click on the link.

Vishing (voice phishing)

involves calls to victims that use a fake identity to trick you into thinking the call is from a reputable organisation. They may pretend to be from a bank and ask you to contact a number (operated by the attacker) and enter your account information. Your account's security gets compromised as a result.

Spear phishing

is a more targeted variation of the phishing scam in which an attacker selects certain persons or businesses to target. They then customise their communications to their victims' features, employment positions, and contacts to make their attack less visible.

Whaling

A whaling attack is also known as a whaling phishing attack. It specifically targets high-profile employees, such as the chief executive officer or chief financial officer, to steal sensitive information. In many whaling phishing attacks, the attacker's objective is to dupe the victim into authorising high-value money transfers to the attacker.

Malware

Malware is a short form for "malicious software". It is a program that infects, examines, steals, or performs nearly any action desired by the attacker when given across a network. Moreover, malware comes in so many varieties; there are countless ways to infect computers. There are many types of malware; we are discussing a few here.

Viruses

Viruses attach their malicious code to clean code and wait for an unwitting user or an automated process to execute it. They can spread swiftly and widely, much like a biological virus, causing harm to systems' basic functions, corrupting files, and locking users out of their machines. Typically, they are contained within an executable file.

Ransomware

Ransomware is a type of malware that encrypts the files or lock-out system of a victim. The cybercriminal then demands a ransom from the victim in exchange for restoring access to the data. Users are shown how to pay a charge to obtain the decryption key. The payments can be thousands of dollars and are paid in Bitcoin to hackers. Ransomware attacks have become very prevalent in recent times affecting individuals to large companies.

Trojan Horse

A Trojan horse is a malware that disguises itself as a legitimate programme and infects a computer. Trojan horses are so named due to the method by which they are typically delivered, which involves an attacker using social engineering to conceal malicious code within legitimate software.

Backdoor Trojans — These Trojans can install a "backdoor" on a user's computer, allowing an attacker to take control of the machine, upload stolen data, and even install more malware.

Downloader Trojans — The main goal of these Trojans is to download more content, such as malware, into the victim machine.

Infostealer Trojan — The main goal of the Infostealer Trojan is to steal data from the infected computer.

Remote Access Trojan — The Remote Access Trojan is designed to give the attacker complete access over the computer.

What is a Backdoor?

A backdoor, in cybersecurity, is anything that allows an unauthorised user to access your device without your knowledge or permission. While backdoors can be installed by software and hardware developers for remote technical support purposes, they are typically installed by cybercriminals or to facilitate access to a device, a network, or a software application.

Backdoors are any malware that allows hackers access to your system. It includes rootkits, trojans, spyware, cryptojackers, keyloggers, worms, and even ransomware. For cybercriminals to successfully install a backdoor virus on your device, they must first find a weak point (system vulnerabilities) or a compromised application in your device.

Some common system vulnerabilities which can cause backdoor on a device/web server include:

- Unpatched software
- Third-party plug-ins
- Weak passwords
- Weak firewalls

Rootkit

A rootkit is a type of computer malware that allows someone to take control of your system. It is pretty dangerous. It's a form of secretive software, usually malicious, meant to keep specific processes or applications hidden from standard detection methods. It enables unrestricted access to a computer.

Keyloggers

Keyloggers are a sort of monitoring software that records a user's keystrokes. One of the oldest types of cyber threats, these keyloggers record the information you type into a website or application and send it to a third party. Modern keyloggers can record screenshots, webcam, chats and your voice through mike too. Hardware keyloggers also exist, which make its detection impossible through any anti-malware system.

Cyberstalking

In the current age, cyberstalking is a new type of digital crime in which a person is stalked or tracked online. A cyberstalker does not physically follow his victim; instead, he follows his online activities to gather information about the person and harass and threaten them verbally. It is an infringement of one's online privacy.

Cyberstalking differs from offline stalking in that it is carried out through the Internet or other electronic methods. Cyberstalkers annoy their victims through email, chat rooms, websites, discussion forums, and open publishing websites (e.g. blogs). The availability of free email, social media platforms and the anonymity afforded by chat rooms and forums has contributed to a rise in cyberstalking instances.

Check your Facebook friends and connections, as well as other social media sites, and narrow down your list to people you actually know. Make sure you control who has access to your profile and information. Block the person who is cyber-harassing you and, if required, report the incident to the cyber cell with digital evidence like screenshots of the messages the person has sent.

DDoS

A Denial-of-Service (DoS) attack is a deliberate attempt by attackers to deny service to intended users. It involves overloading a computer resource with more requests than it can handle, resulting in server overload using its available bandwidth.

A "Distributed Denial of Service" (DDoS) attack is another type of denial-of-service attack in which several geographically dispersed attackers flood the network traffic. DDoS attacks are primarily directed at high-profile organisations' web servers, such as the government or businesses.

A DDoS attack involves multiple connected online devices, collectively known as a botnet, which devastates a target website with fake traffic.

If you use cloud-based services for hosting, you'll almost certainly have unlimited bandwidth. Many of the websites that DDoS harm are those that have little resources. Making the switch to a cloud-based service can help you stay protected.

Spoofing

Spoofing is the act of misrepresenting an unknown source's message as coming from a known, trusted source.

For example, you are a victim of phone spoofing when a caller on the other end falsely introduces themselves as a representative of your bank and requests for your account or credit card information. The most prevalent type of spoofing is email spoofing. In this, the attacker manipulates the sender's identity to convince the recipient that the email is from a legitimate source and instructs them to click on the link provided in the email. Spoofing can apply to emails, caller ID, GPS, Facial images, IP addresses, websites, etc.

Spoofing can be used to acquire access to a target's personal information, spread malware via infected links or attachments, circumvent network access rules, or redistribute traffic to launch a denial-of-service attack.

We will learn to find a spoofed email in the Practice Time.

Identity theft and Credit Card frauds

Identity theft occurs when some cybercriminal impersonates you by stealing your identity to access resources like credit cards, bank accounts, and other benefits under your name.

The imposter may exploit your identity to perform additional crimes. "Credit card fraud" is a broad phrase for crimes involving identity theft in which the culprit funds his activities with your credit card. In its most basic form, credit card fraud is identity theft. The most prevalent type of credit card fraud involves your pre-approved card coming into someone else's hands.

Cryptojacking

Cryptojacking is a type of malicious crypto mining that occurs when cybercriminals get access to computers, laptops, and mobile devices to install the software. This programme mines for cryptocurrencies or steals cryptocurrency wallets from unsuspecting victims using the computer's power and resources. The code is simple to install, operates in the background, and is undetectable.

Cryptojackers can hijack your computer in a variety of ways. When you click on a malicious link in an email, crypto mining code is downloaded directly to your machine. Once your computer gets compromised, the cryptojacker begins mining cryptocurrency around the clock while remaining undetected.

Some Tips to defend yourself against Cybercrime

Let us learn a few steps which you can take to secure yourself and your devices online. You have to do many more things, but these are the necessary things that form the basis of the cyber safety

1. Always keep a legally purchased antivirus programme installed on your PC and smartphone to generate warnings and defend systems from cyber attacks.
2. Create strong passwords by using a combination of upper-case, lower-case letters, numbers, and symbols. Do not repeat your password for your different accounts. You can use a password manager to generate a strong and unique password for all your online accounts. You can also use Passphrase instead of passwords. A passphrase has spaces in-between words.
3. Wherever the option is available, go passwordless. That way, you need to authenticate through prompts on your Cymartphone and do not require entering passwords. DO NOT CLICK ON UNNECESARY AND UNKNOWN LINKS.
4. Always implement 2-step verification for all your accounts. That way, a verification code or prompt on your mobile phone will add another layer of protection to your online accounts.

5. When opening suspicious emails with unknown links or attachments, use caution. Whenever possible, avoid downloading anything from an unsafe or unknown source.

6. After opening a website, check and ensure that you are on a legitimate website.

7. Make sure to keep your PC/Smartphone/Apps/OS up-to-date with software latest updates.

8. Avoid using public Wi-Fi since it is unsafe and unencrypted. Do not log in to your bank account or make a payment on an eCommerce site in a public place.

9. Increase the security of your router and Wi-Fi to protect your home network.

10. Change default login credentials of all connected IoT devices and routers.

PRACTICE Time

1. Hover the pointer over the sender's name

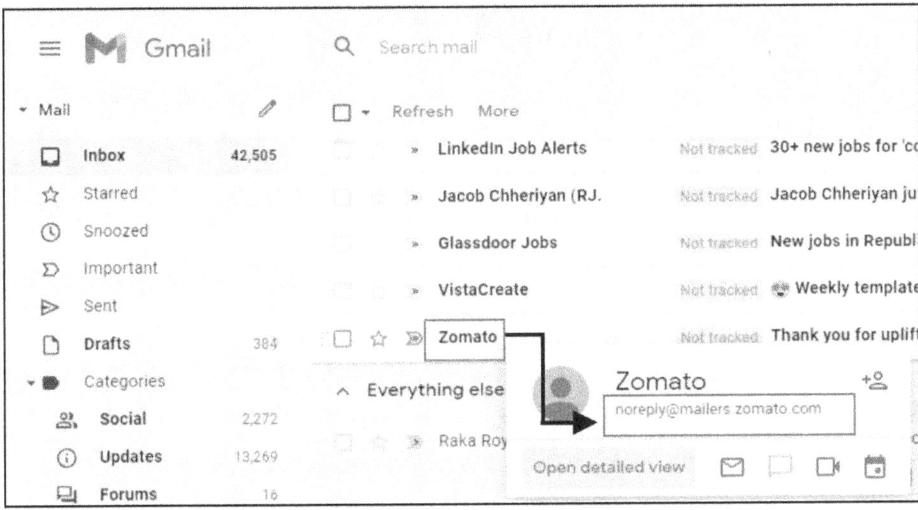

You can see the actual email address from where the email has been sent.

2. Open your inbox and write the email ids of senders of the first five emails you have got in your inbox.

a. ____

b. ____

c. ____

d. ____

e. ____

WORKSHEET

1 **Answer the following questions.**

A. Which one of these cybercrimes involves playing with the minds of users.

a. Malware

b. Social Engineering

c. Phishing

d. Cryptojacking

B. Tick (✓) the names which represents malware.

a. Social engineering

b. Rootkit

c. Trojan

d. Identiti theft

e. Spoofing

f. Virus

g. Ransomware

h. Whaling

2 **Match the Columns.**

	A		B
1.	Spear Phishing	a.	This attack involves multiple connected online devices, collectively known as a botnet
2.	Identity theft	b.	It is a type of malware that encrypts the files or lock-out system of a victim
3.	Keylogger	c.	It is a more targeted variation of the phishing scam in which an attacker selects certain persons or businesses to target.
4.	Ransomware	d.	This cybercrime occurs when some cybercriminal impersonates you by stealing your identity to access your financial resources and other benefits under your name.
5.	DDoS	e.	These are a sort of monitoring software that records a user's keystrokes.

2 Malware Types & Removal

a. Types of malware
b. About anti-malware Software
c. About a 3-2-1 backup plan

About it

The term **malware** consists of two terms, **mal**icious and soft**ware**. Malware is an umbrella term, and there are many types of malicious programs that come under it. A virus is also a type of malware that infect systems by inserting its code into other programs. There are numerous varieties of malware that can harm your computer, and some antivirus applications are only designed to detect a certain sort of software. It is preferable to use software that can identify all or almost all of the numerous forms that malware can take. All latest Antivirus software, despite its name, protects a computer from viruses and provides malware protection in general, but still, it is better to be double sure.

Vijay returned from the office and found her daughter Richa working on the laptop, but seemingly very worried.

It seems like your computer is affected by malware. You should have installed antivirus software on your laptop.
But only yesterday I installed free Antivirus software from a website for my computer.

OK. A free antivirus can be the cause of the malfunctioning of your computer. Most of these free antiviruses are storehouses of malware. It would have helped if you bought legitimate antivirus software from a trusted website. Do you know hackers can activate your laptop's webcam and microphone without your awareness? I hope you have a backup of all essential files.
Oh, That is so scary! Yes, I took a backup of all my important files on my USB drive before installing that free Antivirus.

Types of malware

The list of malware types continues to grow as technology develops, which is why getting the proper malware protection is so important. Here, we are discussing some common types of malware. Buying an antimalware (antivirus) program ensure that it protects against all common types of malware.

Viruses

Viruses need an active operating system or software that is already infected. A virus may remain dormant until the infected host file or programme triggers it. After that, the virus is able to replicate and spread across your system. A virus to infect a system requires a user to click or copy it to media or a computer.

Worm

Worms spread across computer networks by exploiting operating system flaws. A worm is a self-replicating programme that infects other computers without the need for human intervention.

Trojans

Like the Trojan horse, trojans trick users into believing that it is legitimate software. When a user downloads it, the malicious code gets executed. These Trojans can install a "backdoor" on a user's computer, giving the attacker access to the machine and allowing them to manipulate it, upload stolen data, and even install more malware.

Ransomware

Ransomware is a form of malware that encrypts your data and demands payment in exchange for its release. It usually encrypts files on the hard drive or locks down the device and displays notifications requiring the user to pay the attacker to remove the restrictions and regain access to the files. But there is no surety that even after paying the ransom, your files will be decrypted (released). The best advice to protect from Ransomware is to ensure you have a complete offline backup of all critical files. Also, use Windows utility Bit Locker, or these days antiviruses also give the feature of encrypting the drive, so that even if a hacker captures your files, it won't be readable for him.

Spyware

Spyware is also a type of malware. It gets installed on your device without your knowledge and is intended to monitor your internet activity and surfing habits. Activity tracking, keystroke collection, and storing of account information, logins, financial data, and more are all examples of spying capabilities. Hackers can distribute Spyware by taking advantage of program flaws, bundling with cracked software versions, or hiding in Trojans.

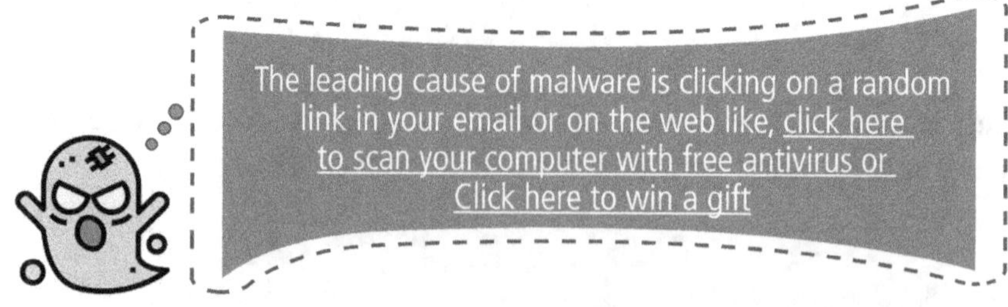

Protection against Malware

Once the malware has infected your file, it is challenging to bring files to their original status. You can never be sure which files have been changed, or the malware hides behind a legitimate file. Antiviruses work best when your computer is clean and you install it at that time. There are some steps to follow:

- Use a trusted, purchased antivirus on your PC as well as the mobile phone. Do not install any free antivirus.

- Schedule the updates for your operating system, browsers, and all applications to install automatically. That way, your computer systems will always have the most up-to-date protections in place.

- Do not buy cracked versions of software, as most of them are pre-activated with malware.

- Install some useful extensions like Netcraft for Chrome browser so that if you happen to open a malicious website, the extension will block it and give you a warning about it.

- Even if you have an effective antivirus installed, you must have a periodic backup taken and stored on cloud storage as well as offline.

- Follow the 3-2-1 Backup Rule for your data. The 3-2-1 backup rule is an easy-to-remember acronym for a common approach to keeping your data safe in almost any failure scenario. The rule is: keep at least three (3) copies of your data and store two (2) backup copies on different storage media, with one (1) of them located offsite, which could be cloud storage also.

About Next-Gen Antivirus

Next-Generation Antivirus (NGAV) employs a combination of artificial intelligence, behavioural detection, machine learning algorithms to anticipate and prevent known and unknown threats.

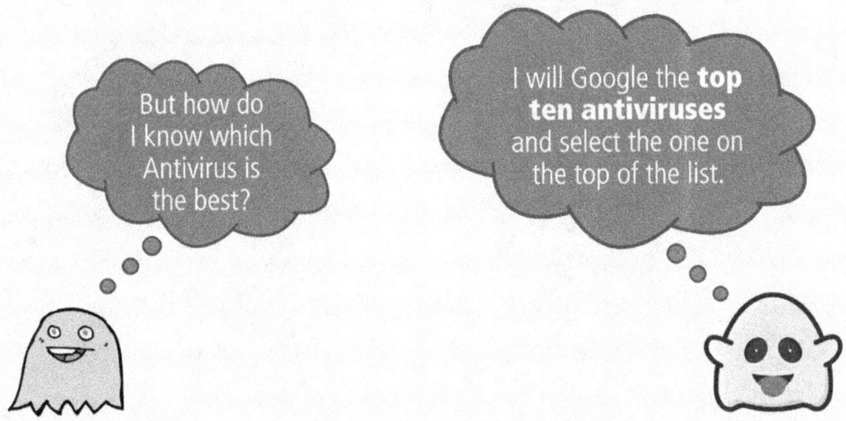

Encrypting your data using an Antivirus (here, we are using Trend Micro Antivirus+)

1. Search and click on the Antivirus program.

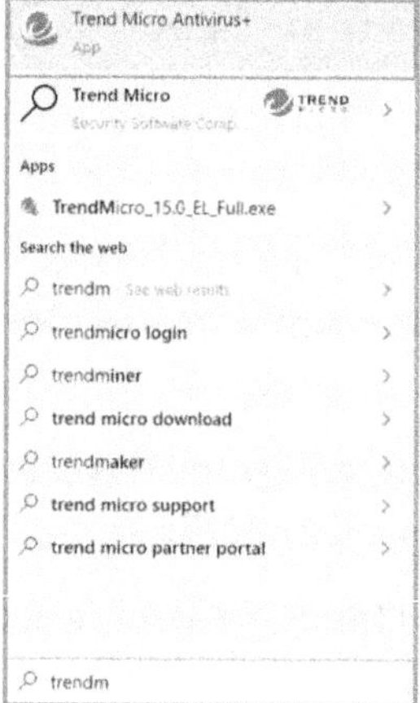

2. Click on the Data icon.

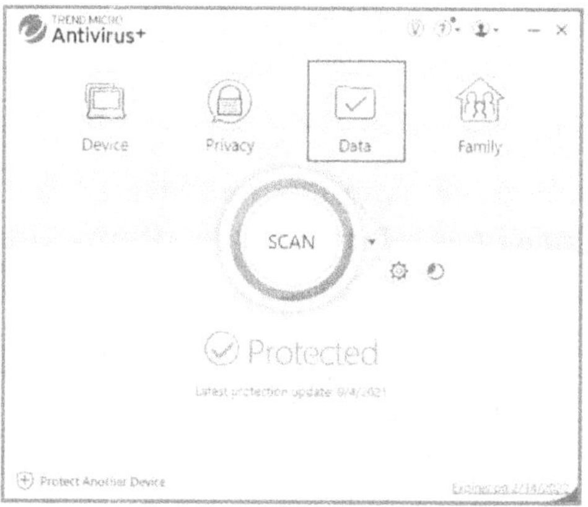

3. Click on the Configure button.

4. Select the Drive or Folders (by clicking on the + sign in front of drives) to protect. Click on the OK button.

5. You can see the selected drive (here, drive F) has been protected.

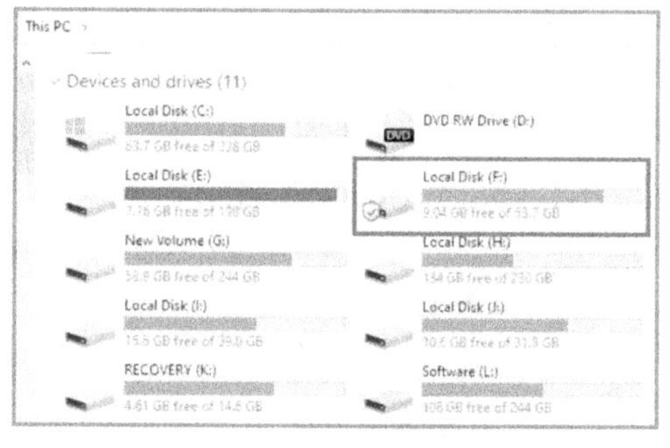

WORKSHEET

a. Which is the correct backup policy?

- ☐ 3-2-1
- ☐ 1-2-3
- ☐ 1-2-3-4
- ☐ 2-1-3

b. Which Chrome browser extension stops malicious web pages from opening in the browser?

- ☐ Carfetner
- ☐ Netcrafet
- ☐ Stopit
- ☐ Netcraft

c. Which of these encrypts your files and do not decrypt them till you make a payment?

- ☐ Trojan
- ☐ Ransomware Virus
- ☐ Spyware
- ☐ Ransomware

d. What is the advantage of a 3-2-1 backup plan?

____

____

3 Creating a Strong Password

a. Steps to create a strong password
b. Using a password manager
c. Know about various password hacking methods

About it

Password managers are applications that help you manage a large number of passwords. They save the login information for the various accounts and automatically fill out the login information in the respected web pages. It helps to prevent eliminates the need to remember multiple passwords.

Password managers create strong, unique passwords for each online account and provide an efficient way to manage all of your passwords. Even if you do not use a password manager, you should know how to create a strong password for your account.

Mitesh was back from the office and relaxing. His daughter Ishi was working on her Laptop. She just created a new account email account for her online classes. Buts he looked worried, and her father noticed it.

No, that is not okay. You should never keep a password so simple as a mobile number, date of birth and your dog's name. It is considered a weak password and can be guessed and found easily by any bad actor.
Then what should I do?

There are some rules to create a strong password. Also, you can use a passphrase instead of a password. Ideally, it would help if you use a password manager.
Dad, please tell me all about this as lots of my friends are also in the same confusion. Also, explain some types of attacks that bad actors use to break our passwords.

Rule 1:   use at least eight characters (take it as a starting point). The more characters you use, the harder your password get guessed by the cracker.

Rule 2:   use a combination of different characters. It should be a combination of uppercase and lowercase letters, numbers, punctuations to special characters like @ and #. Using all of these types of characters can help strengthen your password.

Rule 3:   Never use standard information in your password. Many users use information like birthdate, last name, pet name, phone number, and other related information to make it easy to remember. But it is a bad idea as a cracker can guess it easily.

Rule 4:   Check your password strength. Before applying a specific combination of characters as your password, you can ensure how strong it is to be used as a password. There are several online tools you can use to gauge password strength. One such tool is https://howsecureismypassword.net

Rule 5:   Use a passphrase. A passphrase made up of common words that were put together at random. Remember that a pass could be something like 'pretty glutton legislator shorter monsoon5.'

Rule 6:   When you reset the password, do not set any old password as the new password.

Working of a Password Manager

A password manager is like an encrypted digital safe room that stores your login information for apps and accounts on your mobile device, websites, and other services.

Besides safeguarding your login credentials and sensitive data like credit/ debit card numbers and bank account details, these password managers include a password generator to help you create strong, unique passwords and avoid using the same password in multiple places. The only thing is you to memorize the master password to open a password manager. Make it complex, and do not forget it.

Lastpass, Dashlane, Kaspersky password manager are some excellent password managers.

Types of password attacks

Some of the leading password attacks are mentioned below:

Dictionary attack

A dictionary attack is a method of guessing a password that involves attempting many common words and simple variations. Attackers use extensive lists of the most commonly used passwords or simply words from a dictionary – hence the attack's name. Some letters are also converted to numbers or special characters, such as p@sswOrd.

Brute Force Attack

A brute force attack uses a script to enter combinations of letters, symbols, and numbers during a brute force attack, but these are entirely random. The attack can even use all the characters on a keyboard to create various combinations to try against a password. There is very much possible that one combination will break the password.

Credential Surfing attack

Credential stuffing refers to a hacker's attempt to use previously exposed (stolen) user names and passwords to log in to other websites.

Internet users continue to reuse the same passwords for multiple accounts. They also do not practise strong password hygiene. This makes it easier for bad actors to gain unauthorized access to critical accounts after breaking into a less critical one (like an account on a pizza website, then they will try to access your email/social media accounts). So, never repeat the same password for multiple accounts.

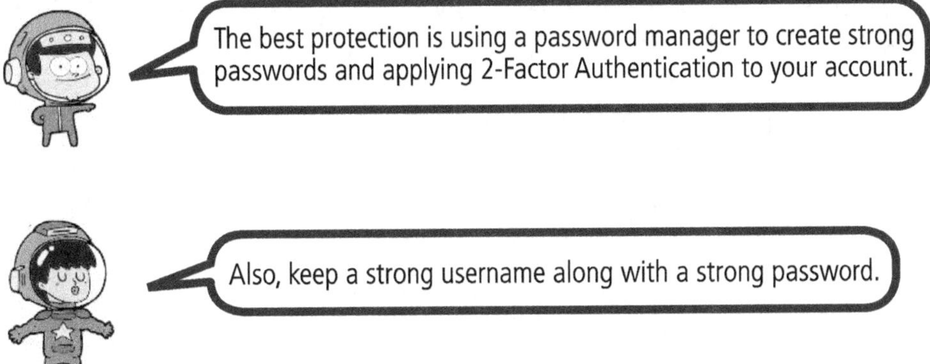

Using the Kaspersky Password Manager (free version)

1. Enter the URL www. kaspersky.co.in/password-manager in the address bar of your browser.

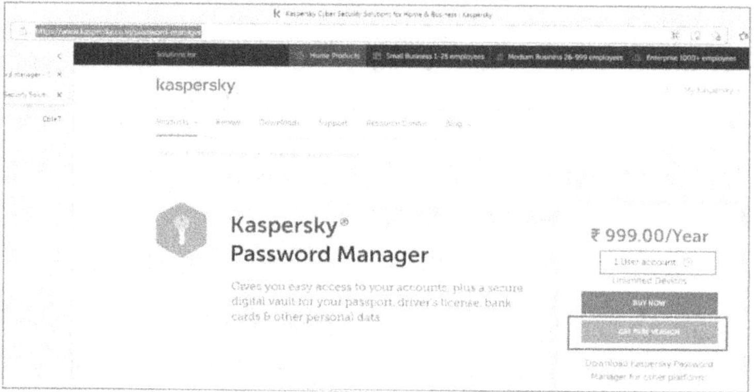

2. Click on the **download for PC** button. Double click on the downloaded file to install the Kaspersky password manager.

3. After agreeing with Terms and Conditions, and registering you will be able to store your passwords in the password manager, and also generate strong passwords.

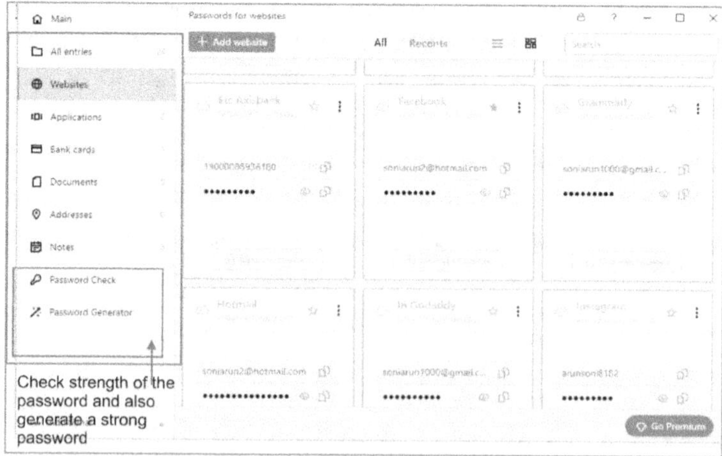

WORKSHEET

Which is the most robust password and why?

- [ ] Heismyfriend
- [ ] 9815204980165744556677990067777
- [ ] Arun@1970%43
- [ ] 5is p@ssw005d 1s v2r90 str0n5

____

____

Match the following:

A	B
Brute Force Attack	In this attack, the attackers use extensive lists of the most commonly used passwords or simply words from a dictionary.
Credential surfing	This attack can even use all the characters on a keyboard to create various combinations to try against a password.
Password Manager	It refers to a hacker's attempt to use previously exposed (stolen) user names and passwords to log in to other websites.
Dictionary attack	This can help create strong, unique passwords without remembering and avoiding using the same password in multiple places.

4. To learn about 2-Factor Authentication (2-FA)

a. Advantage of 2-FA
b. How to apply 2-FA to your Gmail account

About it

Two Factor Authentication (2-FA) is an extra layer of security. In 2-FA, first, a user will enter the username and a password for the online account. Then, instead of immediately getting access, they will be required to provide another piece of information. That information could be in the form of a verification code or Prompt sent on their smartphone.

Bill just turned fourteen. His father gifted him a laptop and a smartphone to attend his online classes and go for tuition without difficulty.

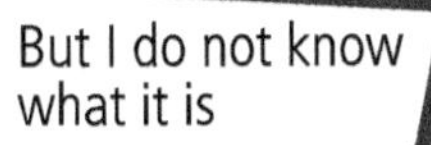
But I do not know what it is

It will link your email account with your mobile number. You will need to complete a second step to verify it's you when you sign in. You will get a prompt on the mobile phone. You can allow the sign in if you requested it by tapping Yes. Otherwise, you tap No.

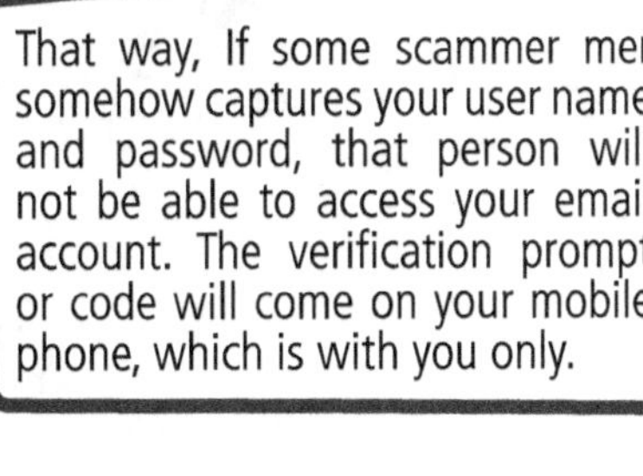
But what is the advantage of that?

That way, If some scammer mer somehow captures your user name and password, that person will not be able to access your email account. The verification prompt or code will come on your mobile phone, which is with you only.

Setting up 2FA on messaging apps like WhatsApp and Signal will protect you if someone manages to swap your SIM. The scammer will not be able to install the messaging service associated with your mobile number on his mobile phone.

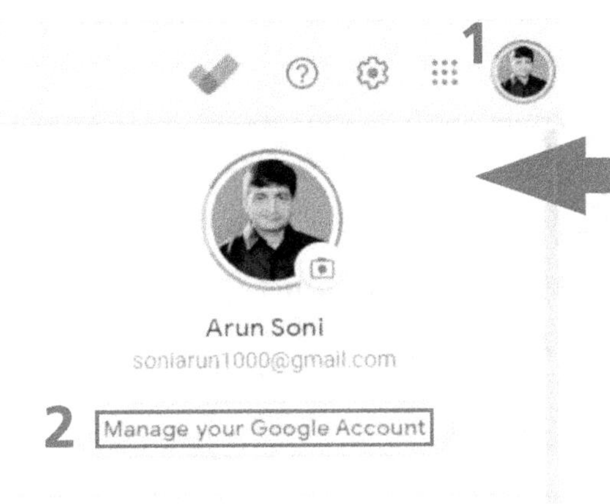

Steps to apply 2-FA to a Gmail account

1. Log in to your Gmail account. Click on the Profile image.
2. Click on **Manage your Account** option.
3. In the navigation panel, select **Security**.
4. Under **Signing in to Google** section, select the **2-Step Verification**.

Follow the on-screen steps.

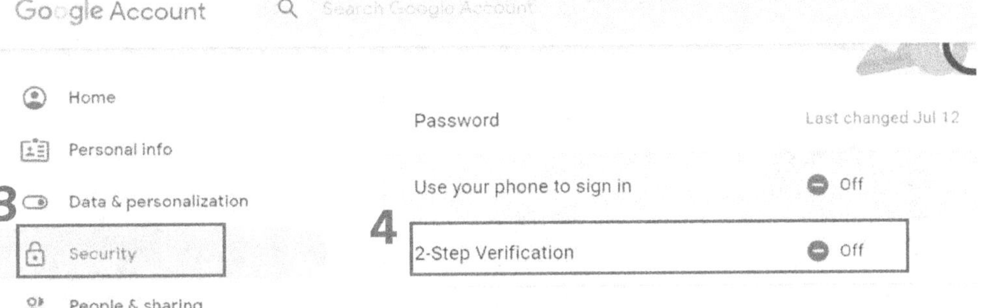

2fA is also known as Multi-factor authentication (MFA). You can get an OTP, Time based OTP (TOTP) and Prompt to verify your account.

WORKSHEET

1 Help Kim to select other names for 2 step Verification by Tick marking ✓ the correct options.

- ☐ 2 Factor Authentication
- ☐ Multi factor Authentication
- ☐ Dual-factor authentication
- ☐ 2 person Authentication

2 Help Aksha to put a cross ✗ against the option which is not a website to check malware in a file

- ☐ Gmail
- ☐ Yahoo mail
- ☐ Facebook
- ☐ Instagram
- ☐ Snapchat
- ☐ Quora
- ☐ Twitter
- ☐ WhatsApp

5 Using Social Media Securely

a. Knowing adverse effects of social media
b. Tips for using social media securely

Ishika and her mother, Sabhyata, were like friends. They used to travel, shop and chat together for hours. Ishika was very active on social media and was part of many groups. She was studying in college and had summer vacations in June. Her father was away for a month on a business trip by chance. So, she and her mother decided to drive to a nearby hill station to spend the weekend. On reaching the destination, after settling in the hotel, Sabhyata saw Ishika smiling and working on her smartphone.

You mean that your location and photographs of us picnicking here are public now. Have you kept the viewership limited to your friend's circle or made it public?
Mom, It is public. Why are you worrying? Now more and more people will come to know about my profile. I want to make lots of friends.
Ishika, Do you have any idea what you have done? A research study shows that most criminals commit crimes like burglary and kidnapping, taking hints from social media. Now the whole world knows that we are both here, and our house is locked and empty back in the city.
Oh God! What have I done !? I will immediately delete the post. I hope till now no wrong person has seen the status and photographs.

Tips for using Social Media Securely

The following tips will make you aware, how to use Social Media.

- Learn how to use the Privacy and security options on social media sites. They're there to help you manage your online experience and keep track of who sees what you submit.

- Be careful of disclosing too much personal information on social networking sites. The more information you provide, the easier it will be for a hacker or someone else to steal your identity and access your personal data.

- Create an open profile or a "fan" page if you're seeking to establish a public persona as a blogger or expert. It will encourage broad engagement while limiting personal details. Use your profile to keep your true friends (those you know and trust) informed about your everyday activities.

- If someone is harassing/threatning you on social media, remove them from your friends' list, block them and report them to the social media administrator.

- Cybercriminals frequently use email links, tweets, postings, and online advertising to try to steal your personal information. If something appears dubious, delete it even if you recognise the source.

- Let a buddy know if something they have posted about you makes you uncomfortable or seems improper. Similarly, if a buddy approaches you because anything you have posted has made them uncomfortable, keep an open mind.

- Do not upload photographs/videos under a challenge, like 'Couple Challenge or any other, as anyone under that particular hashtag (which you used for that challenge) can find thousands of photographs and misuse them

- Always Watermark your photographs and videos before uploading them on social media.

PRACTICE Time

In Privacy check up, go to Settings and Privacy ⟶ Privacy Checkup option to control the profile and post visibility

1. In Privacy Checkup, there are options like 'Public', 'Friends' and 'Only Me'. Use these to control the visibility of your profile components and posts.

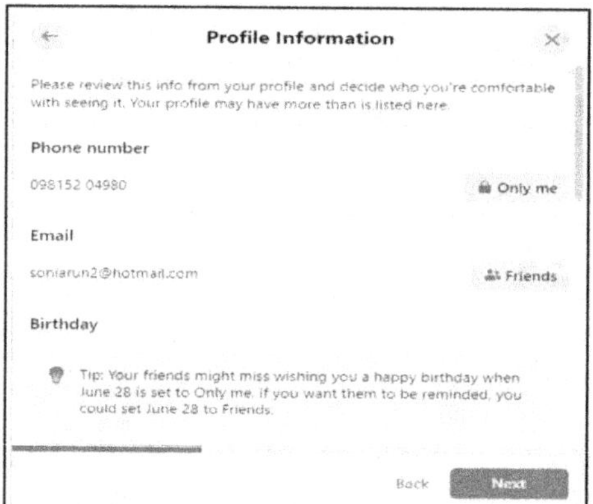

2. Most importantly, it would help to control who can see your posts. There are various options available. Know about all of these.

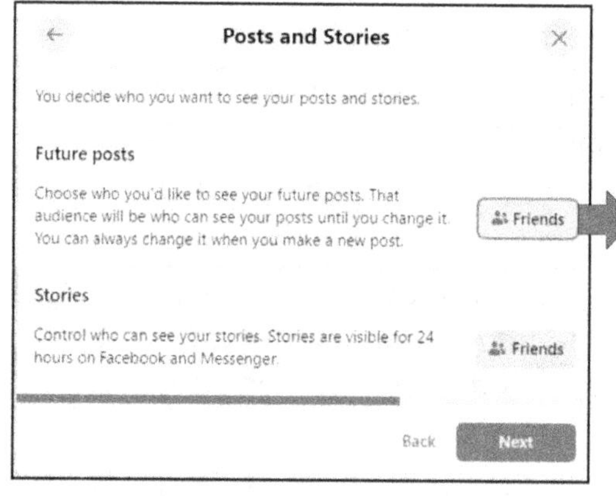
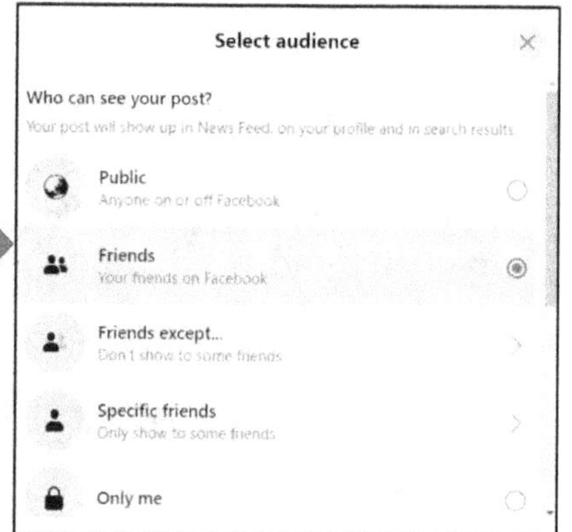

The Privacy Checkup option also let you know how to keep your account secure, Your data settings, and your ad preferences. Do not forget to check all.

WORKSHEET

1 **Tick (✓) the correct options.**

a. Which components of your profile should be visible to the public on any social media platform?

1. Phone number
2. House address
3. Educational Qualification
4. Check-in status

b. All of your posts should be:

1. Public
2. Visible to you only
3. Visible to friends only
4. None of the above

2 **Whichever social media platforms you are using, find out what is in the Privacy option. Write down the name of any two options and what that controls.**

Social Media Platform	Option	What it controls

About it

Cyberbullying is aggressive and maliciously hurtful behaviour directed at another person. Unlike "normal" bullying, which occurs in person, cyberbullying occurs online, mainly through social media platforms, emails and instant messaging services. Sending hurtful, threatening, or offensive messages or images, posting private information about someone else or intentionally excluding someone from an online group are all examples of the act.

Cyberbullying can lead to agonizing fear, low self-esteem, social isolation, and lower academic performance. It can also make it difficult to create healthy relationships, and victims may experience stress, anxiety, and depression symptoms.

Navya's mother reached home after her evening walk. When she entered Navya's room to check whether she had her milkshake or not, she saw that Navya is working on her laptop but seems very tense.

Oh! It is serious, but do not get worried. It is very nice that you told me about it. Did you add any unknown person to your social media account? Let me check your social media account.
No, mom. I did not add any unknown person. Most of them are my school friends. But some connections are from another country where I recently went on a school trip under a cultural exchange programme.

Firstly, what we will do is, block that person. Now that person cannot contact you anymore. Tomorrow, I will go to your school and meet the counsellor. Soon we will find out who is troubling you. Let me take screenshots of the messages which the person is sending. It will form the digital evidence.
Yes, that will be better. I will also tell the names of my friends with whom I had differences. The person could be one of them.

Some examples of Cyberbullying

Listed below are just some examples of cyberbullying

1. Sharing of an embarrassing photo or video of someone on social networks

2. Sending abusive, threatening or vulgar messages and emails to another person or posting them in a forum

3. Spreading rumours about a person to demoralize them

4. Creating a fake profile of someone on social networking sites to damage someone's reputation

5. Excluding someone from a social networking group intentionally to harass a person

How to Prevent Cyberbullying

The following ten points can help you to stop the cyberbullying

1. Do not make your private information public on social media platforms. It can allow bad actors to impersonate you or spread false information about you.

2. Always secure your account with 2- FA and log out after using the account. By not doing so, you risk the bully changing your password and locking you out for an extended period of time.

3. Restrict your online profiles to only trusted friends so that only they can view the information and posts you make public. Do not add random strangers to your account.

4. Writing a clear message to the bully asking them not to contact you is unlikely to stop them from bullying you further, but it will help if you provide evidence to the authorities

5. Avoid using free Wi-Fi, which is normally available at cafes, airports and hotels. If you have to use that, always use a trusted VPN service to access that to prevent passing on login details to bad people.

6. Once in a while, use the Google search engine to search for your name and phone number. Check out how much personal information it exposes. Take actions to remove excessive information about you

7. Don't respond to bullying. Cyberbullies and bullies, in general, thrive on fear and adverse reactions to their abuse. If you don't answer, you may not end the bullying completely, but chances are they'll get bored with you and your lack of response.

8. Block the bully to make sure the bully can no longer contact you on whatever platform they've been bullying you. Share the problem with your parents, teacher or counsellor.

9. You cannot build a case against a bully to the authorities unless you have digital evidence to back up your claim. Take screenshots of the communications, copy them to a document, print them off, and so on. It's usually a good idea to have hard copies of essential documents if something happens to your computer/phone.

10. On a PC, you can take a screenshot of the offensive message using the print screen key of the keyboard (also know how to handle the screenshot on your mobile phone.) Do not delete the emails, messages, chats or anything objectionable sent to you.

11. Learn to collect digital evidence in a tamper-proof way. Prepare yourself for every eventuality in cyberbullying. There can be a short offensive message or ten screens length web page defaming you. If there is a multi-screen lengthy web page or video to capture, use some recording extension like **Nimbus** extension for the Chrome browser.

12. If Cyberbullying is not stopping and affecting your mental health, do not hesitate to report it to the cybercrime cell. It is advised to confine minors to some trustable adults like parents, brothers or sisters. For that, you need to know the website, email id and helpline number of the cyber cell. You also need to provide the digital evidence along with the filing of the report.

13. Report the bullying to the social media help centre. You must know how to and where to report bullying on a social media platform you are using. All have helpline emails and links to register the complaint.

14. Take action if you know someone who is being bullied. Simply being silent encourages an abuser and does nothing to assist. The best course of action is to attempt to end bullying by taking a stand against it. Offer support to the victim. If the individual is a friend, you can listen and decide how to assist. If you are not already acquainted, simply a pleasant word can help lessen the discomfort.

15. The following are some email ids of various platforms to report your abuse to:

Report Abuse to Instagram: *support@instagram.com*

Report Abuse to Facebook: *support@fb.com*

Report Abuse to Snapchat: *safety@snapchat.com*

Report Abuse to Whatsapp: *support@whatsapp.com*

Also, there is a provision in the Help or Contact Us link to report anything nasty to the social media platform. Learn to use the reporting feature so that you don't lose time if you have to use it.

Blocking, unblocking, Restricting a person on Facebook

1. Open the profile of the person you want block. Click on three dots. The person will get blocked.

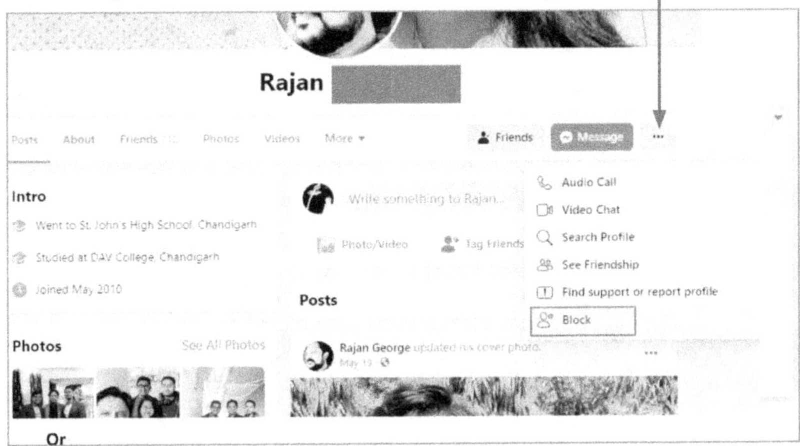

Or

2. In **Settings and Privacy** option, you can Restrict, Block or Unblock the person. Go through all these options carefully

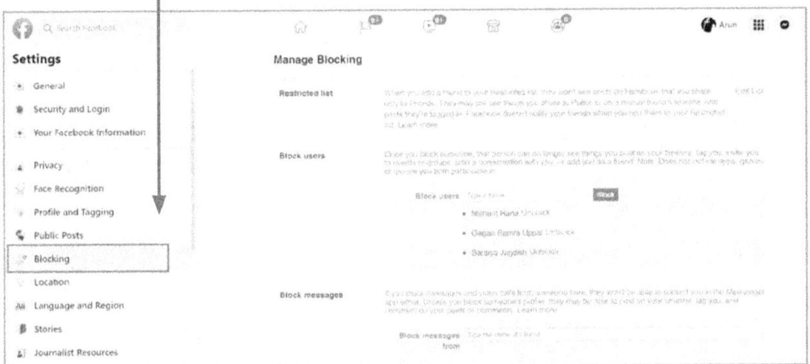

43

WORKSHEET

1 **Suppose someone is cyberbullying you, which of the following is an appropriate thing to do. Tick ✓ the correct answers.**

- [ ] Talk to that person
- [ ] Block that person
- [ ] Switch off your PC
- [ ] Report to the Social Media platform
- [ ] Report to Cyber Crime Cell
- [ ] Start Crying
- [ ] All of the above

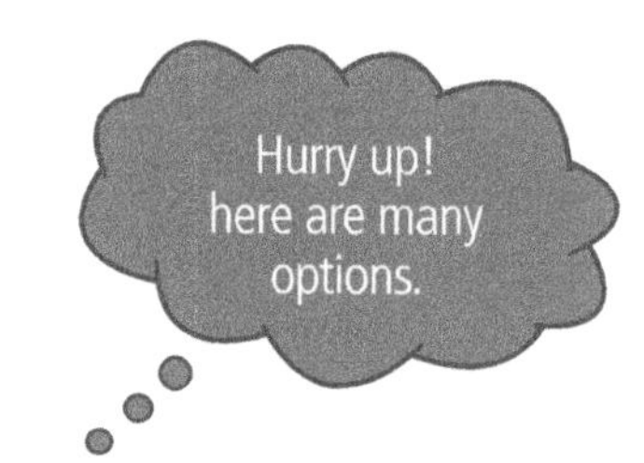

2 **Answer the following.**

a. Write down the URL of the website which deals with cybercrimes in your country. Also, write down the helpline number if there is any.

____

____

b. Suppose someone has created your fake profile on a social media platform, and you want to report it. What will be your action plan?

____

____

E-mail Spoofing

a. Learn to check for a spoofed email
b. Learn to scan for malicious links

About it

Email spoofing is a form of cyber attack. A scammer sends an email that has been manipulated and seems to be originated from a trusted source. The purpose of email spoofing is to trick recipients into opening or respoding to the message. That way, the scammer either installs malware or extracts confidential information like credit card number from the reipient.

After his online classes, David was checking his emails. He found an email from a Pizza making company, claiming to give two pizzas free with the ordering of one pizza. That offer looked very tempting to him.

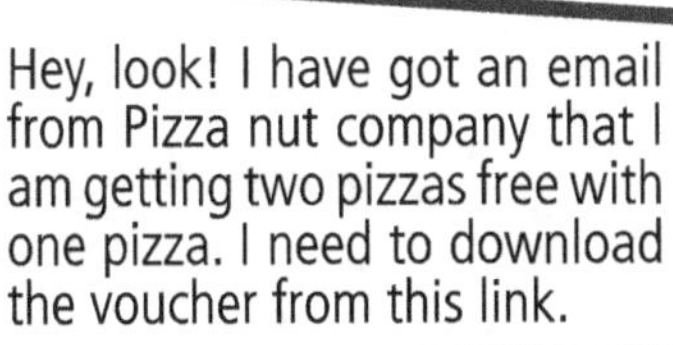

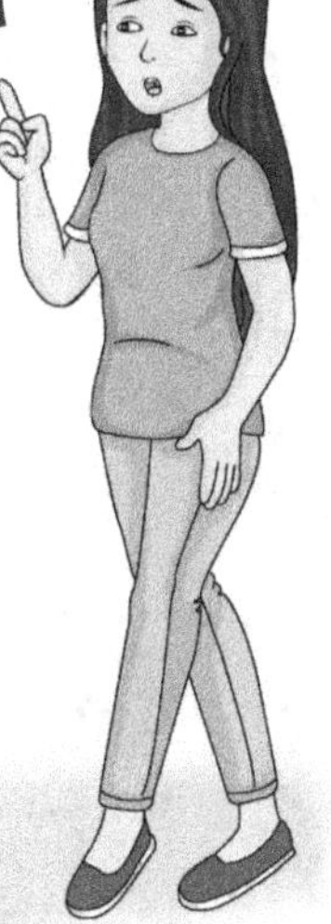

How to do that?

It is simple. Just take the pointer to the sender's name, and you will see the actual email id from which it has come. Look, it is showing xyz@gmail.com, instead of the email address of pizza nut. It is a spooed email.

This email id is okay.

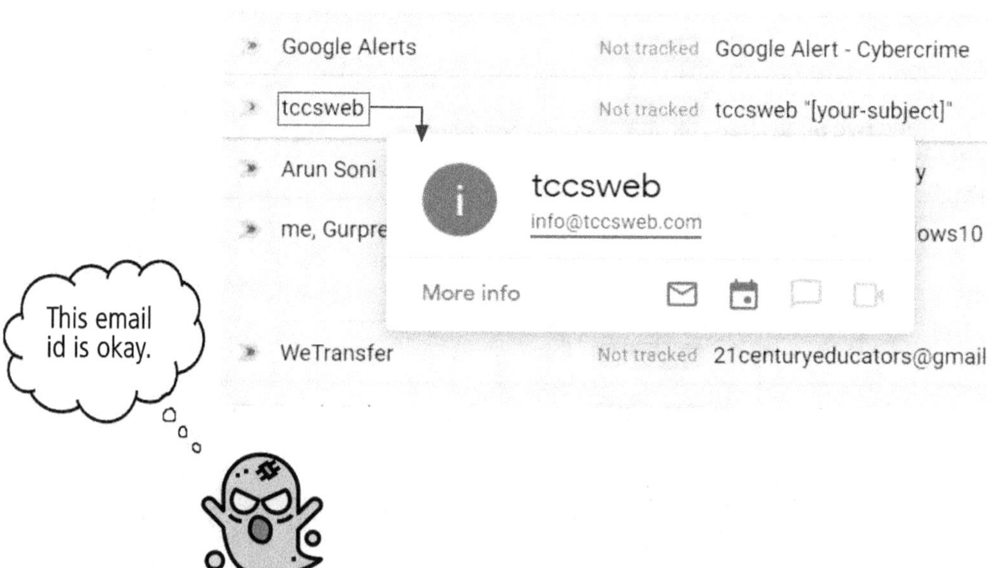
Google Alerts   Not tracked   Google Alert - Cybercrime
tccsweb   Not tracked   tccsweb "[your-subject]"
Arun Soni   y
me, Gurpre   ows10
tccsweb
info@tccsweb.com
More info
WeTransfer   Not tracked   21centuryeducators@gmail

https://www.virscan.org/

https://antiscam.me/

https://virusscan.jotti.org/

https://metadefender.opswat.com/

Https://www.virscan.org/

Upload a file to www.virustotal.com and check its integrity.

1. Go to URL www.virustotal.com

2. Click on the **File** link

3. Click on the **Choose File** button

4. Select the file which you want to scan.

The result

WORKSHEET

1 **Help John to identify and tick** ✓ **the emails which seem to be a spoofed.**

Sender's name		The link shown when pointed to
☐ Amazon	→	info@amazon.com
☐ Instagram	→	info@stagram.com
☐ Pizza nut	→	info@pizzagut.com
☐ Linkedin	→	contact@linkedin.com
☐ Facebook	→	reply@facebook.com
☐ HDFC Bank	→	manager@hdfc1.net
☐ Google Alerts	→	alerts@Google.com
☐ WeTransfer	→	no-reply@wetransfer.com
☐ Pizza Hut	→	contact@pizzahut.co.in

2 **Help Aksha to put a cross** ✗ **against the option which is not a website to check malware in a file.**

- ☐ Gmail
- ☐ virustotal.com
- ☐ jotti.org
- ☐ jotti.com
- ☐ virscan.com
- ☐ Quora.com
- ☐ defender.com
- ☐ totalvirus.com

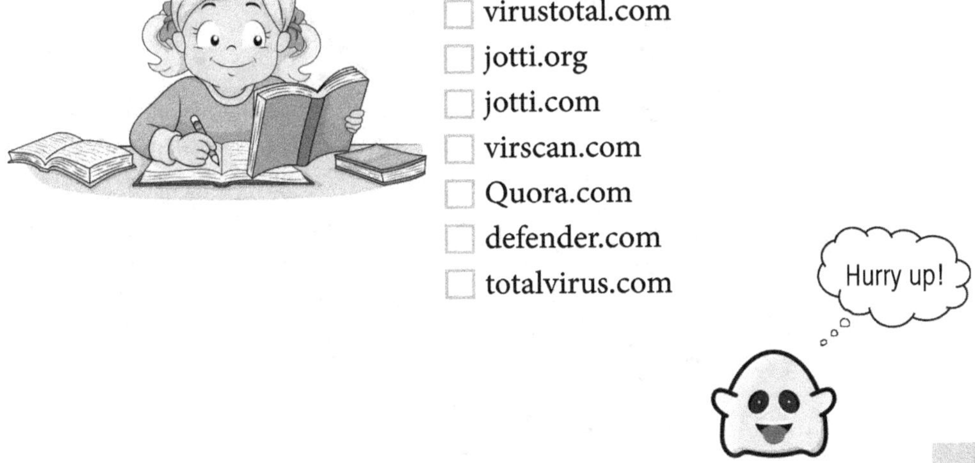

All About IP Addresses

a. Public and Private IP addres
b. IPv4 and IPv6 IP addresses
c. Tracing Geolocation details from an IP address

About it

IP is an abbreviation for "Internet Protocol," a collection of rules that govern the format of data transferred over the Internet or a local network. IP addresses, in essence, are the identifiers that allow information to be transmitted between devices on a network: they contain location information and allow devices to communicate with one another.

Public and private IP addresses are two vital aspects of your device's identity that most people overlook. However, with a significant increase in employees working from home and cybercrime on the rise, it is now more crucial than ever to understand how your device's IP address can expose your identity on the Internet. Remember that whenever you connect to the Internet, a public IP address is assigned to your device.

Romi is a curious teenager. His father, who is an IT professional, recently bought him a Laptop. Now he has lots and lots of queries to ask his father. So, on Sunday, his father decided to sit with him to answer some questions he had in his mind. His father was happy that without being told, he was asking the right question. It means he was learning out of curiosity.

Private (internal) addresses are not routed on the Internet, and no traffic can be sent to them from the Internet. They are only supposed to work within the local network

More about Public IP addresses

A public IP address is one that can be directly accessible via the Internet. It is assigned to your network modem/router by your internet service provider (ISP). Your device also has a private IP address that is hidden when you connect to the Internet using your router's public IP address.

IPv4 Vs Ipv6

IPv4 is a version of the Internet Protocol that is commonly used to identify devices on a network by employing an addressing system. In 1983, it was the first version of IP deployed for production on the ARPANET. IPv6 is the most recent version of the Internet Protocol. This new IP address version is being introduced to meet the increased demand for Internet addresses.

How to find your public IP address?

You can find your public IP address just by visiting the website like www.whatismyipaddress.com, www.whatismyip.com and www.ip8.com.

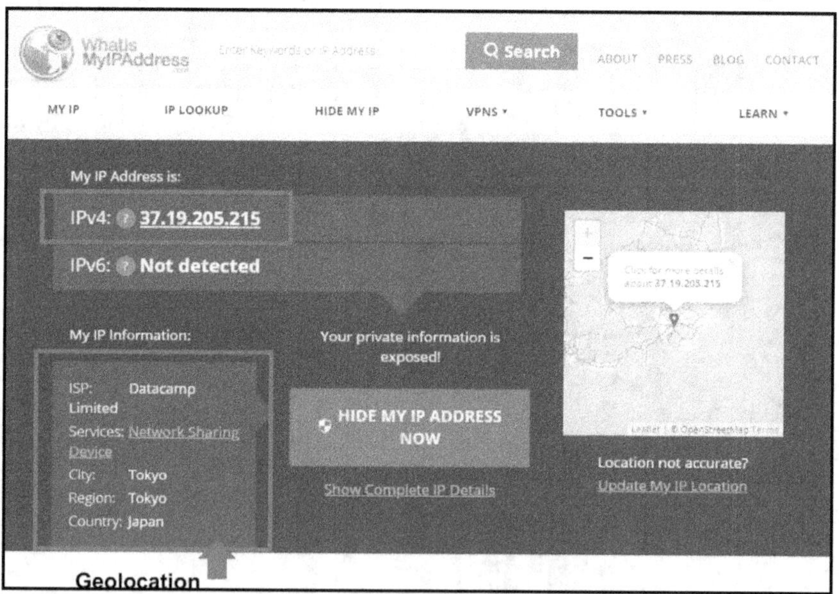

More about Private IP addresses

A private IP address is an address assigned to your device by your network router. Each device on the same network is given a unique private IP address (also known as a private network address) – this is how devices on the same internal network communicate with one another.

Other devices can trace the private IP addresses of a device on your local network. Each device connected to your local network has its own private IP address, which other devices can only see on that network.

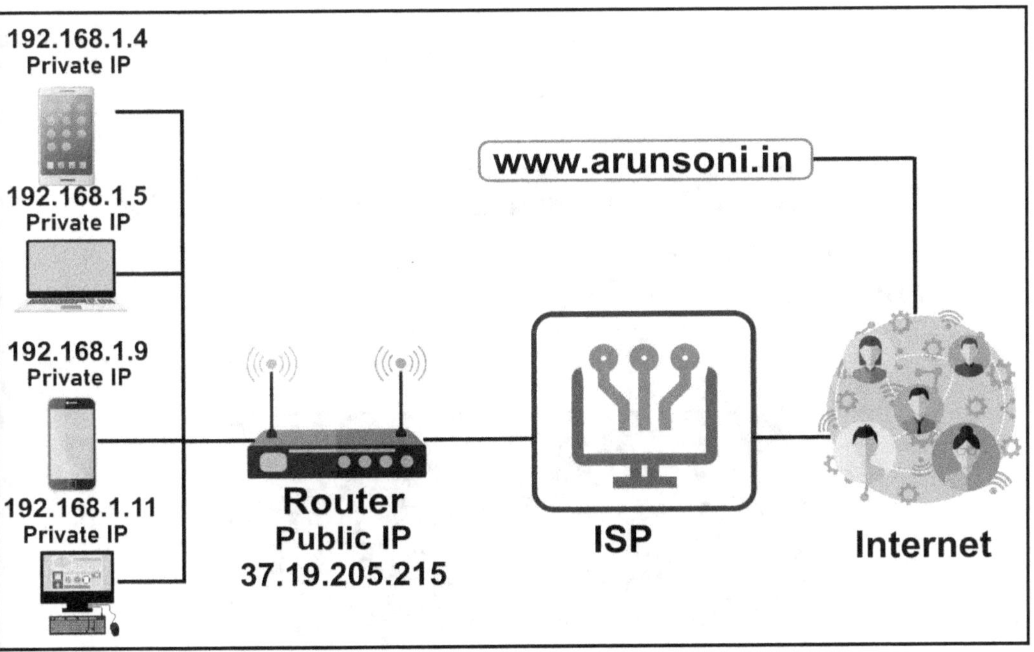

You have found an IP address (49.36.225.128) of someone. How to find that person's Geolocation?

1. Open the website www.whatismyipaddress.com. Click on **IP Lookup**

2. Enter the IP address whose Geolocation you want to find. Click on **Get IP Details**

3. The Geolocation of the IP address you entered will be displayed.

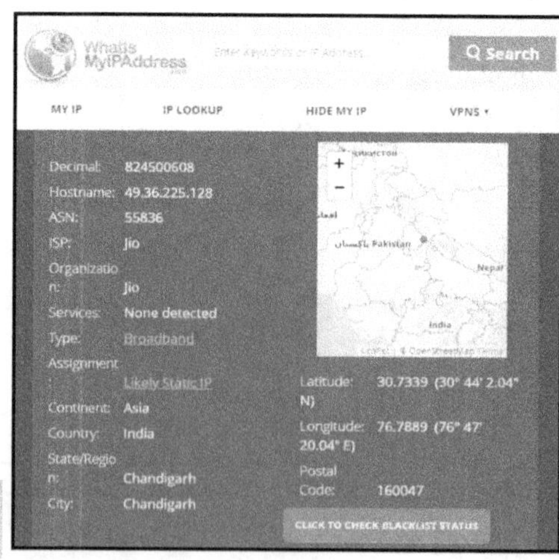

WORKSHEET

Write the name of objects against arrows

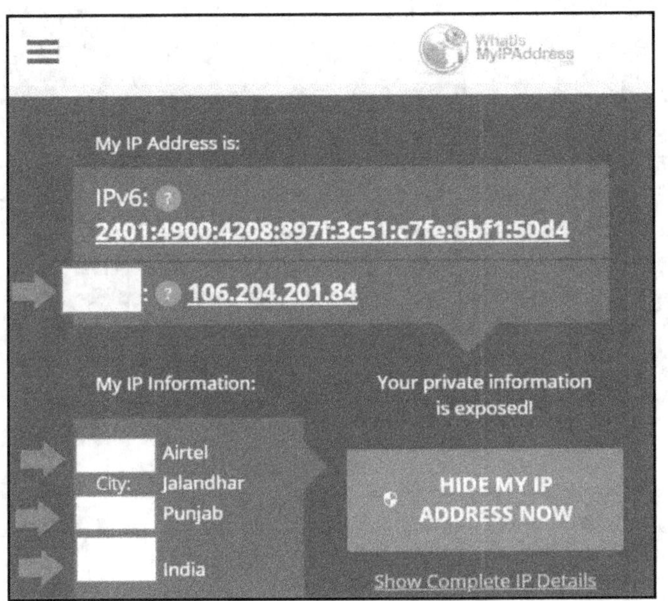

Type in Google search engine 'What is my IP address?' Write down the result

____

____

____

____

9. Default Login Credentials Vulnerability

a. What is the Default login details vulnerability?
b. Finding default login vulnerability in a router
c. Resolving the issue

What is Cybercrime?

Many hardware devices and their accompanying software include a username and password (credentials) that administrators can use to configure them. After the device has been set up, it is recommended that the administrator update the default credentials to something more secure and complex. However, those built-in credentials may remain in place for various reasons, including convenience or forgetfulness.

The attacker who wants to hack your infrastructure will often examine your network for weak points. A vulnerability scan can indicate whether apps and devices are still using their default passwords.

A simple online search will usually disclose the default credentials for a specific product. That's all the hacker needs to gain control of the device. A hacker can potentially obtain access to your device's authentication panel and try the default credentials. The attacker can utilise the access to get into other accounts and servers if the compromised device or application is connected to a server.

Before going any further, you must know the following points:

- A modem is a device that receives an analogue signal from your internet service provider (ISP) and translates it into a digital signal that your devices can understand and vice versa.

- A router is a computer networking device that manages the data entering and leaving the network and data moving inside of the network.

- Modem brings the requested information from the Internet to your network, whereas router distributes the requested information to your devices.

- With today's technology, you no longer need a separate modem and router, as new combination modem and router units combine the functions of the two devices into a single powerful gadget commonly referred to as a "Router." In small offices and homes, we have this combination that makes access possible for all your devices to connect to the Internet.

Arun is a Cybersecurity Expert who conducts seminars & workshops on Cybersecurity to spread awareness against cybercrime in schools and colleges. He is a fast friend of Sunny George. One Sunday, he visited the family of Sunny George. Incidentally, Sunny had bought a new laptop a few days back and installed the broadband Internet connection because due to Covid, he has to work from home. His daughter Ishika was also attending online classes from the same laptop. After some formal conversation, Arun noticed the laptop.

Wow! Sunny, you bought a new laptop with an Internet connection. I think it has the latest processor. I hope your service provider has changed the router's default username and password.
Thank you, Arun. Yes, the laptop will also let Ishika attend her online classes. But, I am not sure whether the engineer who installed the router changed the default credentials or not. How can I check? Would you please help me?

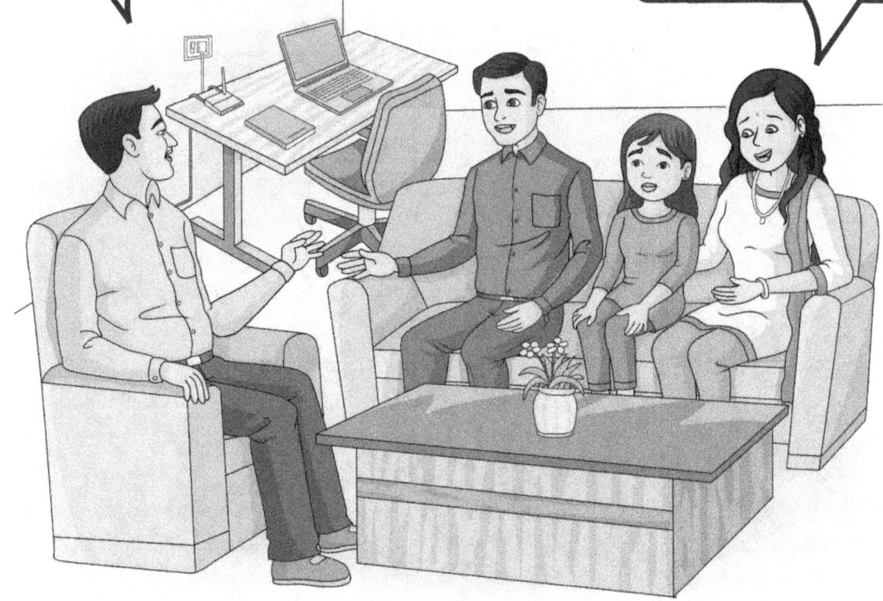

Sure, I will find it out. You must not know that it is the most significant vulnerability in homes and offices where the Internet is used. The technical person installing the router does not change the default credentials in most cases. It can lead to hacking of all your devices connected to your Wi-Fi, and more can happen.
It is worrisome. Would you please check the laptop and solve this issue?

Sunny and Ishika went away so that Arun could work without any disturbance. Arun was testing and checking everything for the router vulnerabilities.

After something appears on the screen, Arun calls Sunny and Ishika to show that on the monitor.

Now, Sunny, I have changed the default login credentials to something complex and noted them down in the diary. I hope you have also seen how to change those.
Thank you, Arun. Ishika and I have observed and will do it ourselves when required. I am also planning to install IoT devices in my house. I will make sure I also change their default credentials.

Fortunately for attackers, many IoT device users never update their device's default passwords once they've set it up, and the device manufacturer rarely encourages them to do so.

Resolve the problem

One of the first things a hacker looks for on a device is if the default account and password are enabled. Many websites list the default credentials for a wide range of devices, old and new, including routers, printers, phones, and even smart toasters.

If you find any devices with their default credentials, the following steps are recommended.

1. If necessary, change or disable default credentials as soon as you notice them.

2. Make sure that fresh passwords are unique, long, and contain a wide range of numbers, characters, and symbols.

3. Don't re-use passwords.

4. Store the new unique passwords safely in a password manager. You can also create strong passwords using the password manager.

To change the check security of your router against the default credential vulnerability

1. In the Search box of Windows 10, type 'command'

2. On the command prompt, type 'ipconfig'

3. The IP address in front of 'Default Gateway' is the private IP address of your router.

4. Open your web browser and enter the IP address in the address bar. Press the Enter key. You will see the authentication box of your router.

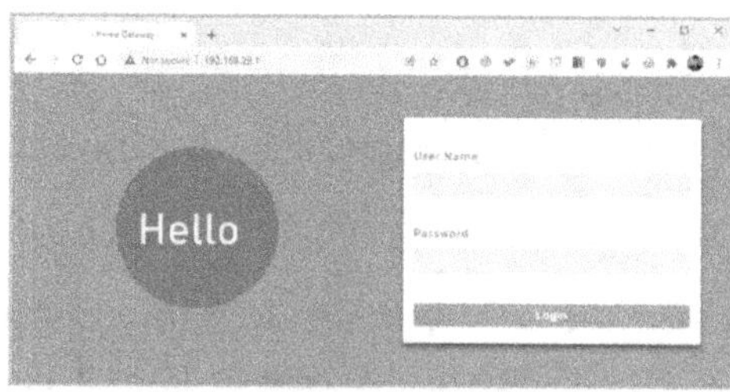

5. Try entering login/user combination admin/admin or admin/password. If the router settings do not open, try finding the default credentials from the web (https://www.routerpasswords.com/) by the manufacturer's name and model of your router. Enter the same in the authentication box. If the Router settings open, it means your router's default credentials have not been changed and is at risk of hacking.

WORKSHEET

1 **Answer the following questions.**

A. Which one of these is not the common username/password combination for default credentials for a router?

   a. admin/admin

   b. admin/password

   c. admin/1234

   d. admin@197#/pass9826%$3@

B. Which one of these is a common IP Address for your router?

   a. 192.168.0.1

   b. 192.168.1.1

   c. Both of the above

   d. None of the above

2 **Fill in the blanks.**

A. Please find out the IP address of your router and write it down

____

B. Visit the website https://www.routerpasswords.com/ and observe how different manufacturers use the most common credentials. Please find out the most commonly used default credentials and write them down.

____

10. Securing Online Teaching/Video Conferencing

a. How to select an online teaching platform?
b. Securing an online teaching session

COVID-19 has resulted in the closure of schools worldwide. Over 1.2 billion children worldwide are not in school. As a result, the whole education system has undergone dramatic changes, most notably the rise of e-learning, in which instruction is conducted remotely and via digital platforms. The benefit of online education is that it can connect students and teachers from all over the world. Your geographic location does not dictate which classes you can enrol in.

However, not all educators are ready to embrace the sudden shift to online platforms. They are unsure which online teaching platform to choose as there is an abundance of these available now. Even if they can select a platform, they do not know how to use the full features so that they can conduct the class securely. As a result, unauthorized users create disturbances in the session by unnecessary screen sharing, file sharing or displaying something objectionable to participants. So it has become an utmost necessity to understand which online teaching platform to choose and how to secure your teaching session?

Three ladies are sitting and talking to each other. Those ladies are teaching in three prestigious schools in the city. But now, due to Covid-19, the schools closed, and now they are teaching through online teaching platforms. Each of them was facing some issues.

How to choose an online teaching platform

If you decide to buy an online teaching/video conferencing platform for your organization, you must think in the following terms:

- The bulk of the platforms accessible requires software installation or a browser plug-in, which can be difficult for some people. Not all users have the necessary technological skills to carry out those processes. An excellent online learning platform should allow users to access the system via a link that can be accessible on any available browser and device, including a desktop, laptop, mobile phone, tablet, and even a smart TV. However, there should also be security features to keep out unwanted participants. Every institute should consider an easy-to-use platform when looking for the ideal platform.

- You must be comfortable with the interface, the functions and the level of control over the class. The tutors may be able to include various multimedia files like PPT, videos, PDFs, and other formats when preparing digital lessons and the Whiteboard feature is there.

- More interactive possibilities, such as sharing webcams, raising hands, emoticons, and virtual tricks, add a user-friendly interface to a learning platform.

- The learning platform should provide complete control over the content of the school and tutors, as well as protection from unlawful use and distribution. The option to delete, alter media files, and limit the participants to share files and screens should be there.

- The platforms should be strongly encrypted so that no unauthorized person can eavesdrop or interfere in an unauthorized manner. Look for the reputation and origin of the company from which you are buying the online learning platform.

Steps for conducting a secure online class

After buying an online platform, ensure that you follow the given points for conducting a secure online class or conference meeting.

- When scheduling your meeting, generate a random Meeting ID and require a passcode to join. You can share these details with the appropriate attendees in private.

- Turn on waiting rooms, which give you more control over who gets into your classroom.

- As a default, disable screen sharing and file sharing. Only hosts should have permission to share screens and contents. They should be in control to switch off someone's video anytime. It will prevent any undesirable, annoying, or improper by any participant.

- Assign a co-host to assist you or continue the meeting if your connection is lost.

- Lock the meeting once it starts so that no user can enter after that. When you lock your session, it prevents more attendees from joining until you admit them.

- The chat feature should be under the control of the host. He should be able to limit the ability of participants to converse with one another while your meeting is in progress, reducing distractions.

- To safeguard the privacy of their living settings, consider requiring or encouraging students to utilize backdrop photos (assuming the online learning platform supports it).

- Be aware that students from countries that restrict the free movement of information and ideas in your class may be vulnerable to monitoring, harassment, political repression, or criminal penalties if they break local laws. Governments in several of those countries are keeping a close eye on the substance of internet communications.

- Install new security features by updating software regularly. The majority of these programs/apps include automatic update capabilities.

- Educational authorities of some countries ban the usage of particular online learning apps for security reasons or lack of trust. Use only those apps which are allowed in your countries.

It is essential that if you host a meeting, then after the meeting is over, you END the meeting. When you do so, the session will end for everyone right away. It is a great way to make sure your students don't hang around in your virtual classroom after you've left.

PRACTICE Time

1. Open your web browser and type www.meet.google.com

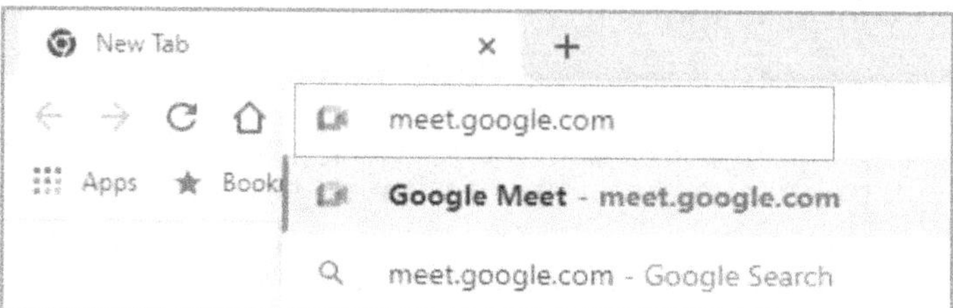

2. Click on the **New meeting**

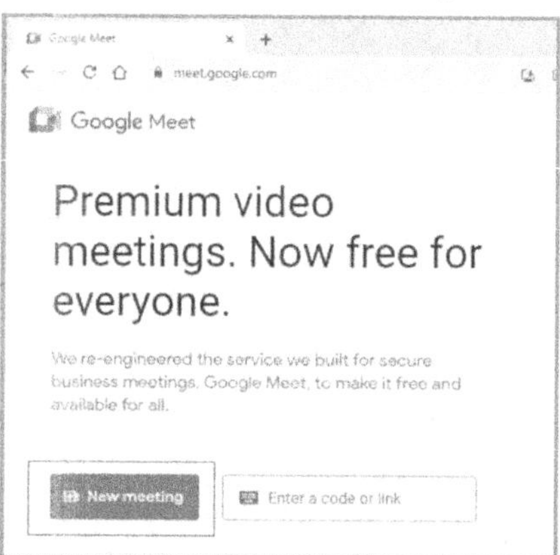

3. Click on the **Create a link for later**

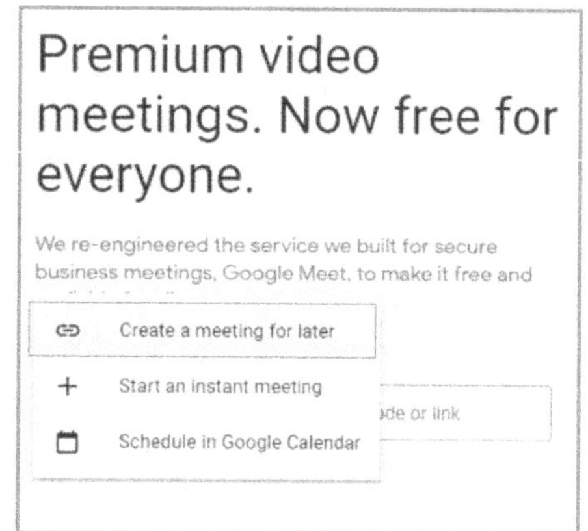

4. The link for the meeting will be generated. Click on the Copy button, and you can share this link with participants. They need to log in from their Gmail account and click on the shared link to attend the meeting.

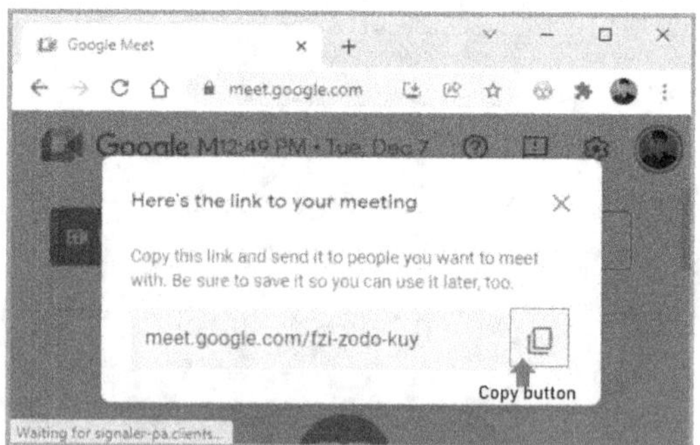

WORKSHEET

1 Find out the name of the company which owns the online teaching/video meeting application and the country where their head office is situated. Also, find out which of these allow screen sharing? Also, give marks (out of 10) to the company's reputation.

Application name	Name of the company	Country	Reputation (in marks)
Google Meet			
Zoom			
Web Ex			
GoToMeeting			
Microsoft teams			
Skype			

2 Find out which online teaching/video meeting applications have Whiteboard features, Screen sharing, and end-to-end encrypted.

Application name	Whiteboard	Screen Sharing (Y/N)	End to end encryption (Y/N)
Google Meet			
Zoom			
Web Ex			
GoToMeeting			
Microsoft teams			
Skype			

11

Mobile Phone Security

a. Securing your mobile phone
b. Steps to check and change permissions of an app

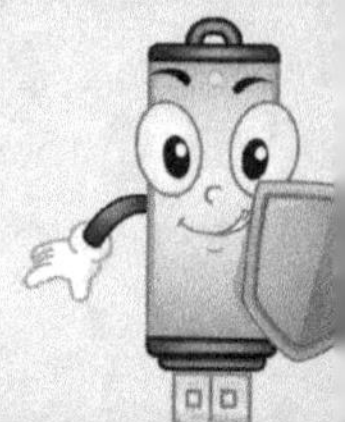

Mobile security is a precautionary measure taken to protect against a wide range of threats that steal information stored on your phone. Mobile phone attacks can steal your personal information, such as bank account information, login information, Photographs, data and even chats on messaging platforms. We can never be sure about the integrity of the apps we download on our phones. Without robust protection in place, these malicious apps, if they get downloaded, can wreak havoc on your phone and hack your data. So smartphones these days have become very vulnerable to cyber-attacks.

Tina and Sheeba are best friends. They study in the same college and are also neighbours. In the evening they often go for a walk. But today, Sheeba was worried about something. When Tina asked, Sheeba said something had happened with her other friend Srishti. The whole incident was making her uneasy.

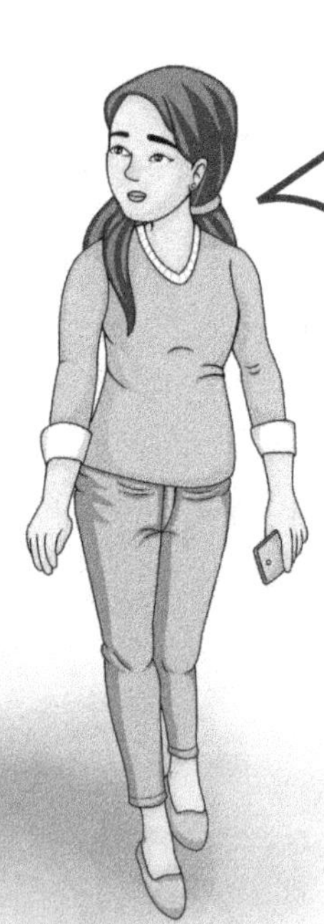

Tips to safeguard your Mobile Phone

Tina told Sheeba ten steps to secure her mobile phone.

1. Do not install apps other than the official app store like Google Play Store (Android) or the App Store (iPhone).

2. Even these app stores can host malicious App, so have a legally purchased antivirus for your phone for complete protection.

3. Only give the required permissions to apps. If an app is asking for non-required permission, do not download it.

4. Beware of Apps that ask permission to access your microphone and camera. These apps can always listen to you and watch you.

5. Always have a screen lock (pin, pattern, or biometric fingerprint) on the phone. Do not leave your mobile phone unattended with anyone you do not trust.

6. Before downloading an app, read its reviews and check the reputation of the manufacturer company.

7. Learn to use <u>Find My Device</u> for Android and <u>Find my iPhone</u> for your Apple products. Check its features which enable you to lock/wipe/track the phone remotely.

8. If you are using WhatsApp, implement 2-step verification and a fingerprint lock.

9. Also, check from where you have/had logged in (applicable for all apps where you have to log in to use)

10. Have a camera blocker app like (Cameraless) to prevent unauthorized use of your phone camera. Or buy a webcam cover for your laptop or mobile camera cover.

PRACTICE Time

To install Netcraft extension in your chrome browser. (Netcraft Extension chrome extension is Complete site information and phishing protection when browsing the web).

1. Go to Settings of your Android phone (here, using the Android 10 version) and tap on the **App**.

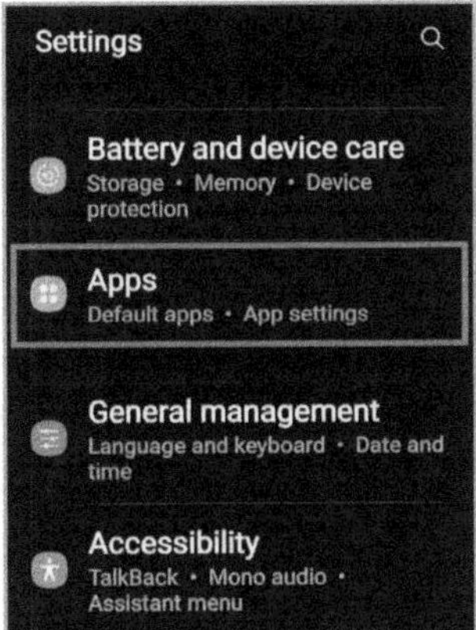

2. All installed apps will be visible. Click on the App (here, AR Emoji) whose permission you want to check or change.

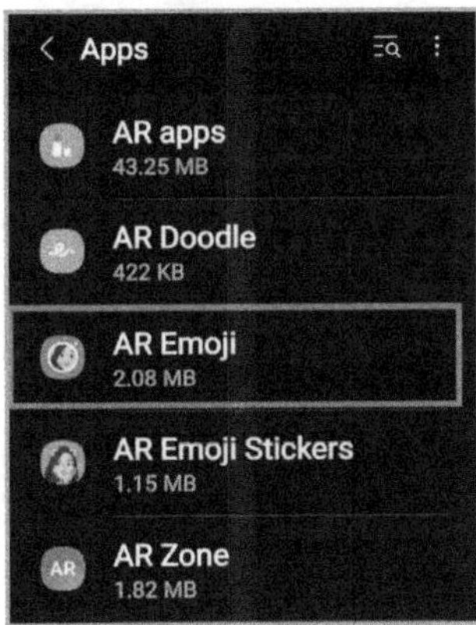

3. You can see the permissions of this App. Click on the **Permissions** to change any permission (here, we are changing the permission of the camera)

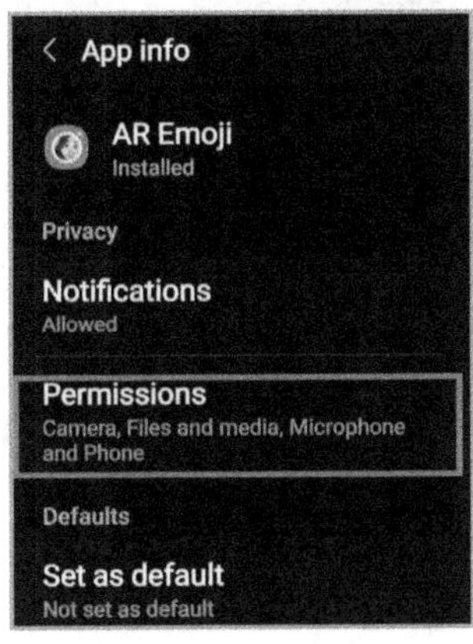

4. Now from here, you can change the permission of the App.

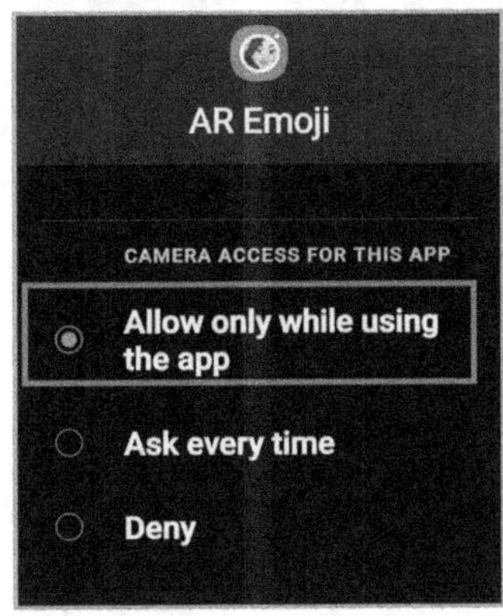

You can also go to the **Settings → Privacy** (like camera or microphone) option to check which particular permission is used by which apps.

WORKSHEET

1 **Answer the following.**

1. Select (✓) or reject apps (✗) after looking at the permissions they require.
   a. Fast food company app – permissions (SMS, Camera, Contacts)
   b. Clock (No permissions allowed)
   c. Dictionary (contacts)
   d. Gmail (Calendar, Contacts and Files and media)

2. Check and fill in the permissions of the following apps on your mobile phone
   a. Facebook ____
   b. Google Play Store ____
   c. Chrome browser ____
   d. Google search engine _____________________________________

2 **Cross the non-required permissions.**

1. A Torch app is asking for the following permissions.
   a. Contacts   __________
   b. Microphone   __________
   c. Camera   __________
   d. Files and Media   __________

2. Calculator app is asking for the following permissions.
   a. SMS   __________
   b. Microphone   __________
   c. Camera   __________
   d. No permissions required   __________

12

All about securing Wi-Fi and VPNs

a. Dangers of free Wi-Fi
b. Securing your Wi-Fi at home
c. Advantages of using a VPN

About it

You may need to access important files on your company's network if you work remotely. You also many times use free Wi-Fi in Hotels, Airports or Cafes to connect. This type of information necessitates a secure connection for security reasons. VPN (Virtual Private Network) services connect to private servers and employ encryption methods to reduce data security risks. A VPN service encrypts the data as well as disguises your identity to secure your data and make browsing a private experience.

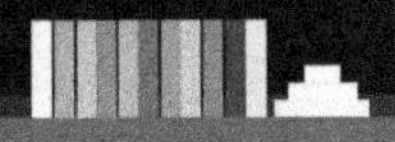

Yuvi was a regular visitor to a café near his house. He often used to take his laptop with him to work there. One day his friend Shivani also accompanied him. She was amazed to see that Yuvi was accessing his social media accounts, using net banking and sending emails to his friends using the free Wi-Fi of the café.

Why so? I think high-speed free Wi-Fi is an excellent option.
Yuvi, I think you never heard of Man in the Middle attack. The bad actors can steal your data when you are accessing your online accounts. It could be through interfering with networks or creating fake access points that the attacker controls.

Oops, I never thought of it. I am immediately disconnecting. What can I do so that I can keep on using the free Wi-Fi without the fear of any interception of my data?
You can use a VPN to secure your information. A VPN encrypts your data so that no one in-between can read it. It also hides your IP address. Hiding an IP address means no one can know about your actual location.

What is a VPN?

A VPN (Virtual Private Network) allows you to connect securely over the Internet. VPNs can be used to access region-restricted websites, protect your browsing activity on public Wi-Fi from prying eyes, and much more

VPNs encrypt your internet traffic and disguise your online identity by changing your IP address. For example, if you are working from India, you can make other people believe that you are working from Canada.

Some reputed VPN Services are :

* Express VPN * Nord VPN * Cyber VOGhost * Hotspot Shield

Man In The Middle Attack (MITM)

A man in the middle (MITM) attack occurs when a scammer inserts himself into a conversation between users and applications. The scammer can eavesdrop or impersonate one of the parties giving the impression that a regular exchange of information is occurring. An attacker can perform this MITM attack in many ways.

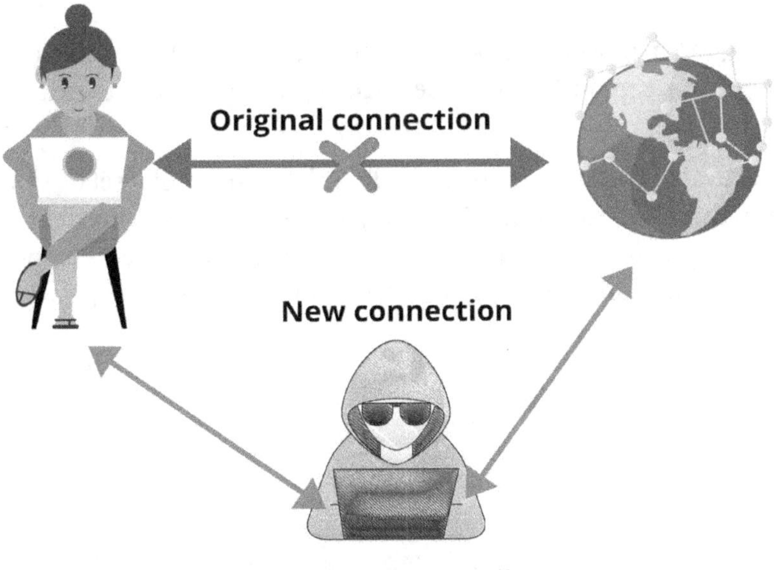

Man in the Middle

Evil Twin method

Devices with wireless cards will frequently attempt to connect to the access point with the strongest signal. Attackers can create their own fake wireless access point (with the same name as the original Wi-Fi name (SSID) and trick nearby devices into joining their access point. It is the simplest form of a MITM attack.

Interception method

When an attacker discovers a vulnerable router (which usually happens in the case of free Wi-Fi), they can use tools to intercept and read the victim's transmitted data. The attacker can then insert sniffing tools between the victim's computer and the user's websites to capture login credentials, banking information, and other personal information.

Wi-Fi Protection

You can take the following steps to counter MITM and securing your Wi-Fi at home

1. Make sure you visit websites that begin with HTTPS and not with HTTP. HTTPS is a sign that the website is secure and can be trusted. The data transmitted through it is encrypted.

2. You should avoid connecting directly to public Wi-Fi routers without the use of a VPN. A VPN encrypts your internet connection while using public Wi-Fi to protect the private data you send and receive while using public Wi-Fi, such as passwords, net banking or debit/credit card information.

3. A strong encryption protocol (preferably WPA3) on wireless access points prevents unauthorized users from joining your network simply by being close by.

4. It is essential to change your router's default login details (set by the router's manufacturer.) If attackers discover your router's login credentials, they can redirect your DNS servers to their malicious servers. It means you will open your bank's website, and some phishing web pages will open.

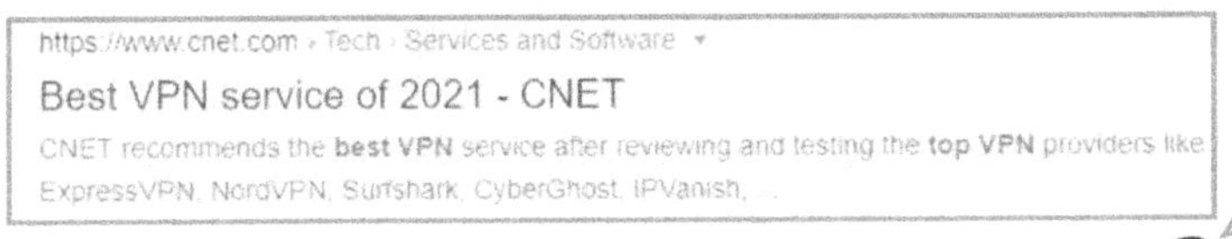

To Select and use a VPN service.

1. Type' top 10 VPN in 2021' in the Google search box.

2. The search results(links) will appear. Click on a trustable link.

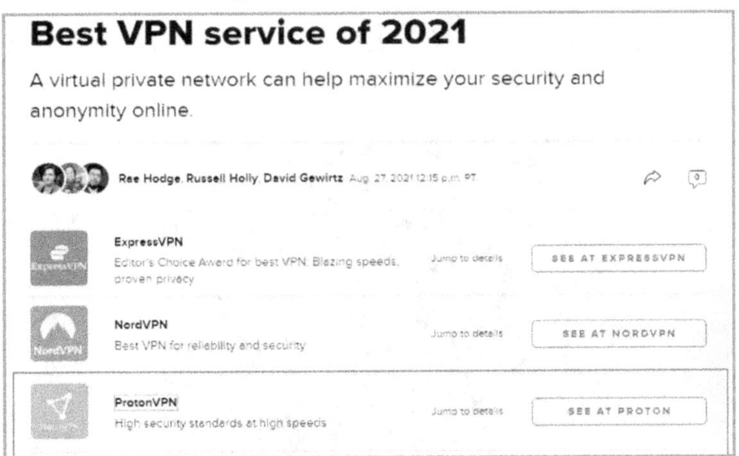

CNET (short for "Computer Network") is an American media website that publishes reviews, news, articles, blogs, podcasts, and videos on technology

3. Open the VPN services displayed and compare their features one by one. Here I am selecting the Proton VPN, as it is a reputed VPN, has a No Logs policy, and offers free service (of course, features get limited in a free version). For my requirement, these features are okay.

4. For getting a free VPN, options get displayed.

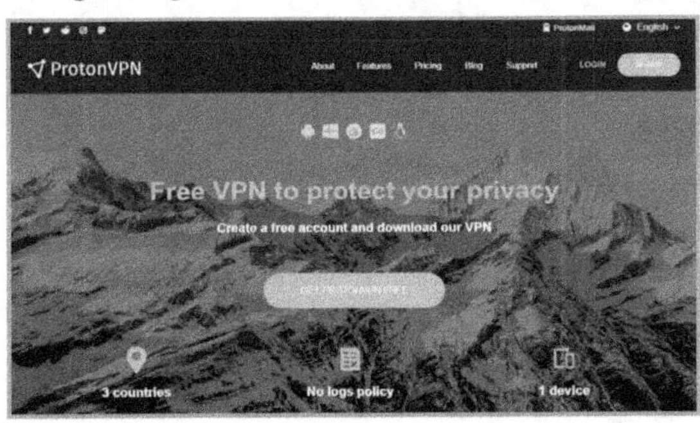

5. Click on the **Pricing** option in the menu bar. Compare the pricing and options provided. The thing to note is that the more servers a VPN has in more countries, the faster the access time will be. (Here, we will click on **Get Free** option). Create an account by clicking on the **Sign Up** option.

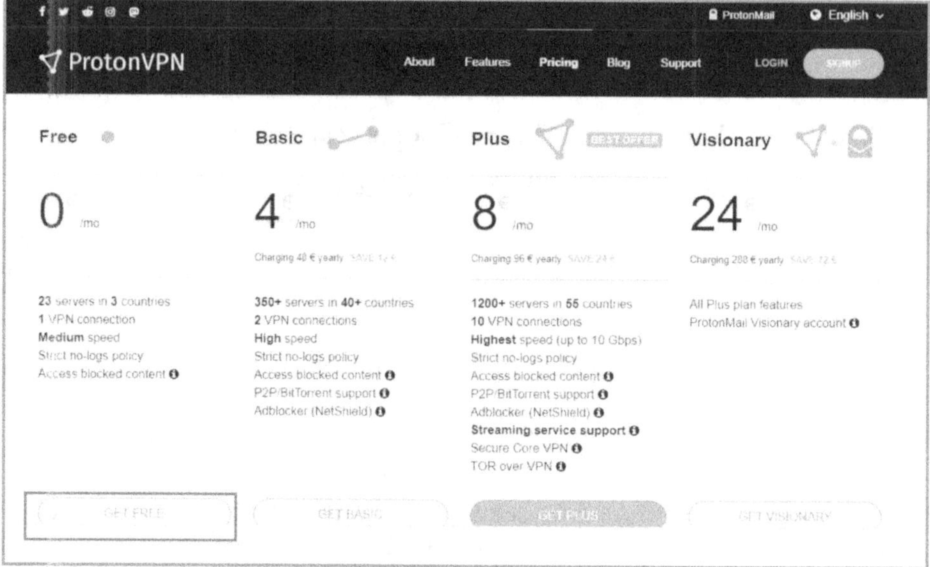

6. Login to get access to the VPN. Select the country now you want your IP address to come from, and click on the **Quick Connect**

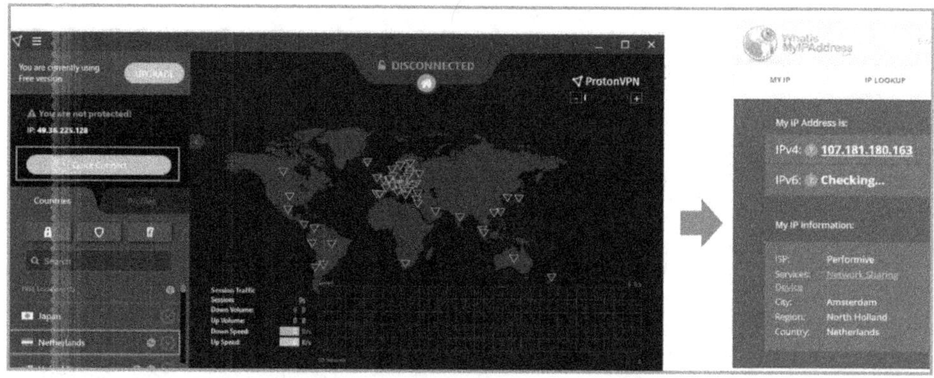

7. **You can check your IP address from a website like** www.whatismyipaddress.com. You will see that your Geolocation is Netherland.

WORKSHEET

 Tick ✓ the correct answers.

a. Which is not a function of a VPN?

☐ To encrypt the data
☐ To disguise your identity
☐ To make your data travel fast
☐ To secure your data from prying eyes.

b. Which is not a feature of a good VPN?

☐ Kill switch
☐ No Logs Policy
☐ Servers in various countries
☐ Slow transmission of data

c. What do you mean by default login details?

☐ The login details set by the manufacturer
☐ The login details set by the ISP
☐ The login details changed by yo
☐ The password set by the manufacturer

2 **Match the following**

1	Evil Twin	A	A Wi-Fi encryption protocol
2	Nord	B	Your online identity
3	WPA2 or WPA3	C	A type of MITM attack
4	Default login details	D	A VPN service
5	IP address	E	Login details set by the manufacturer

Answers: 1 _______ 2 _______ 3 _______ 4 _______ 5 _______

13 Essential Smartphone Safety Apps and More

a. Essential Smartphone Safety Apps for Women
b. Tracking the lost smartphone and securing it

About it

Every home is concerned about the safety of women family members. With the giant leaps that technology is taking every day, security is now at our fingertips. Numerous safety apps can be used on smartphones by women. Integration of SOS facility, GPS and marking of Safe Zone prove immensely beneficial for the users. Most of the apps work similarly. The user can either shake their phones or press the SOS button in the app or press the power button a few times (or even scream) to alert registered contact numbers through text or call. The location of the user with the alert message will reach the registered contacts. Even the police can also be alerted at the same time.

Today Marisa's examination result got declared, and she passed with distinction. Her father bought her a smartphone as a prize for her. She is in a hurry to use that smartphone.

Recommended apps for Android phones

1. *Smart 24x7 personal Safety App* by Smart24x7 - For Android and iOs
   Link: http://bit.ly/3qJIorV

2. *My Safetipin: Complete Safety App* by Safepin
   Link: http://bit.ly/3ug7VNb

3. *TrackiGPS-Track Cars, Kids, Pets, Assests & More* - Tracki
   Link: http://bit.ly/3ug7VNb

4. *CitizenCop* - Quacito / INFOCRATS
   Link: http://bit.ly/3aGs9rn

5. *Chilla- Woman safety app with scream detection* By Kishly Raj Products
   Link: http://bit.ly/3pHvqLBSafe

6. *Safe Family Circle* - RT Tijerina
   Link: http://bit.ly/3khwEvN

Recommended apps for iphones

My Safetipin- Active learning Solutions
Link: http://apple.co/3sdxbBI

Tracki GPS - Trackiinc
http://apple.co/3bq8pHK

CitizenCOP - Quacito/INFOCRATS
Link: http://apple.co/3alp5v7

Safemily Family GPS Locator INVODEV
Link: http://apple.co/3qDjdZs

All these apps can also be used by the Elderly. In case they are outside somewhere and any health emergency occurs, these apps can immediately send an SOS message to their family members.

Features of these APPs

There are so many apps and we have selected a few. Still new apps keep coming up. You must compare the following features before selecting an app.

Alerts: These apps allow the user to choose one or more contacts from the contact list as emergency contacts. When panic action is taken, alerts are sent to these contacts. Alerts can be in the form of location and sometimes surrounding noises and videos.

Geofencing: It is an area on the map where the user is expected to be. When the user steps outside of this area, an alert is sent to the emergency contact. This area can be specified by parents or user of the app.

Methods of sending alerts: Some apps allow you to send an alert by shaking your phone, pressing the power button twice, or pressing the panic button in the app interface. There may be instances where such alerts are triggered without your knowledge. Choose the app that you believe will result in fewer false positives.

Look for permissions: Apps may request personal information or access to data on your phone (such as location, contacts, and photos). If an app requests information that you are hesitant to provide, consider not using it and use another app.

Know the third party: Many times, alerts are sent to a third party who is expected to respond to the alert. Third party can be like police station control rooms or call centres of the app. Before installing the app, know precisely who these third parties are. Some apps also post an emergency alert on the Facebook wall or any other person using the same app nearest to your current location.

Tracking your lost phone

Most Android phones now come with a built-in **Find My Device** feature. This service automatically tracts your phone's location. Using this service on an Android phone enables the **Find My Mobile** option in your phone's Biometrics and Security Settings. Similarly, the iPhone also the **Find My iPhone** feature

How it works?

Find My Device/Mobile will try to find the location of your phone and display it on the map. Provided that it manages to track your phone, it will offer you three options to choose from- *Play Sound, Secure Device* and *Erase Device.*

Even if the phone is in silent mode, it will begin ringing for a few minutes in order for you to locate it if nearby or to alert passers-by.

Additionally, you can choose to secure the phone by locking it and can display a message on the phone for whosever finds it.

In cases as a last measure where it is very hard to rescue a lost phone, the Erase device option will let you delete all data on it.

PRACTICE Time

**Suppose you are not able to find your Android phone.
Track your missing Android phone by following the given steps.**

1. Pick up a PC or a smartphone of your friend, log in to your same Gmail account with which you were logged-in to your android phone.
2. In the address bar of your browser, enter **google.com/android/find**. The location of your phone will be displayed on Google map with the following three options.

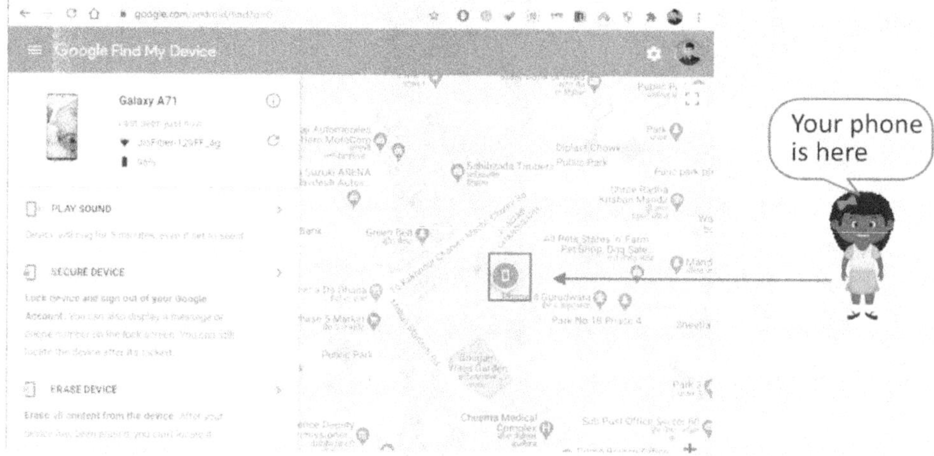

3. a. **Play sound:** You can play a sound so that it makes noise (even if you had put it on silent mode).
   b. **Secure Device:** You can secure your device so that the finder can't access your home screen. This feature is most helpful if your phone wasn't previously secured with a screen lock.
   c. **Erase Device:** You can erase your phone. It is the best option if you know for sure that you aren't likely to retrieve your phone. Remember that after erasing, you will not be able to track it.

WORKSHEET

Help the happy ghost tick ☑ only those names that are of safety apps.

- [ ] CitizenCop
- [ ] Snapchat
- [ ] Tracki GPS
- [ ] My Safetipin
- [ ] Chilla
- [ ] Instagram
- [ ] Safe Family Circle
- [ ] PubG
- [ ] Safetypin

2

Which options you get while tracking your Android phone online? ☑ the correct ones.

- [ ] Play Music
- [ ] Play Sound
- [ ] Create PIN
- [ ] Secure Device
- [ ] Vibrate Device
- [ ] Erase Device
- [ ] Call my Dad
- [ ] None of the above

14 Caring for your Digital Footprints
a. Creating a positive footprint
b. Methods to find your footprints on the Internet

Your digital footprint is a digital record of all of your internet interactions, including your search history, emails, personal information entered on websites, social media posts, and even social media conversations (like comments or likes). It is like a path left behind as you click through the Internet. "How can I delete my digital footprint?" you might think. Unlike a trail of physical footprints left in sand or dirt that eventually washes away, your digital footprint can last indefinitely. It is nearly impossible to entirely delete something off the Internet after it has been posted.

Understanding your digital footprint allows you to pick and control what you leave for others to find on the Internet.

John and Tim were fast friends, and they often used to come to each other's house to study. They used to solve assignments together, play cricket, and do many other things. Every Saturday, they used to go to one or another's house for a night stay. This Saturday, they decided to gather at Tim's house to explore social media. But Saturday was also the day off for Tim's father. When both started using the Laptop, Tim's father was nearby and overheard them by chance.

Hey, You both naughty young men, I heard you. What are you planning to do?
Yes, Uncle, we are just going to have lots of fun today.
Dad, so many of our classmates on this social media platform. We are planning to create some fake profiles of them and send Friend's requests to others. Also, we will make some fake profiles from the name of strangers and have some fun.
I am worried about what both of you are planning. I am afraid that will create harmful digital footprints for you and make you cybercriminals. Based on this, reputed colleges and universities can refuse admission to you.
Cybercriminals! Refuse admission. So scary !!?
What are Digital footprints? Dad, please tell us more?

89

Because the Internet makes it so easy to access and share this information, it's essential to understand and evaluate your digital footprint whenever you share photos and videos, make posts and comments, or converse online. Even when you delete it, you can never be sure the platform where you posted will also delete it.

What can Harmful Digital Footprints Do to You?

If you are not cautious about what you post on the Internet, be ready to have the following consequences.

Damage to reputation

Potential employers, colleges, universities, and others can search your name online and access portions of your digital footprint. If that inappropriately presents you, it could hurt your prospects of getting a job or being admitted into a college or university.

Refusal for scholarships

As part of the online application process, many scholarships ask applicants to reveal their social media identities. Any inappropriate post or otherwise objectionable content spotted on your profile could prevent you from receiving a scholarship.

Internships

In addition, college internships are increasingly becoming a requirement for obtaining post-college employment. Internships are already competitive. Your digital footprint may set you apart from other applicants.

Bullying and Harassment

Information found in a digital footprint be used to harass or abuse people. Somebody can also share and save it for malicious purposes.

Scamming

The more personal information you disclose online, the easier it is for predators to gather information. They can use that information to defraud you or others through identity theft and other methods.

As a parent or teacher, what you can do

Consider the following points while teaching children about creating positive digital footprints.

- Encourage children to use blogs, photos, videos, and community participation to share their good actions.

- Demonstrate how cautious you are about what you do online and how you manage your digital presence.

- When sharing information online, it's crucial to think about your personal safety and privacy and remember to think about the privacy of others. It's a good idea to ask friends and family members whether it's acceptable if you share a photo of them.

- Sit down with your child and search for images and words using their name in a search engine. If you're both unhappy with what you find, either delete the content yourself or respectfully ask the individual who uploaded it to do so.

- Explain to them that they may be exposing a lot of data to that new website (whatever site it is) when they quickly log in using their Facebook or Gmail account. It's usually safer to sign up for new websites with a secondary email address rather than allowing this level of access.

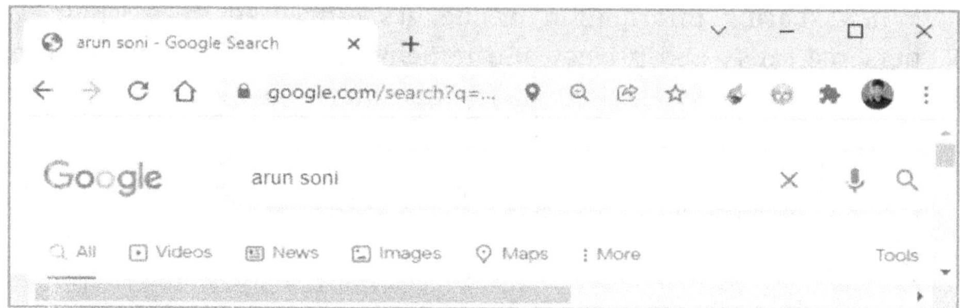

PRACTICE Time

To search for your digital footprints on the Internet using Google Search Engine.

1. In the Google Search Engine, search for your name.

2. Look for the links which appear. Click on the links which you think are pointing towards you.

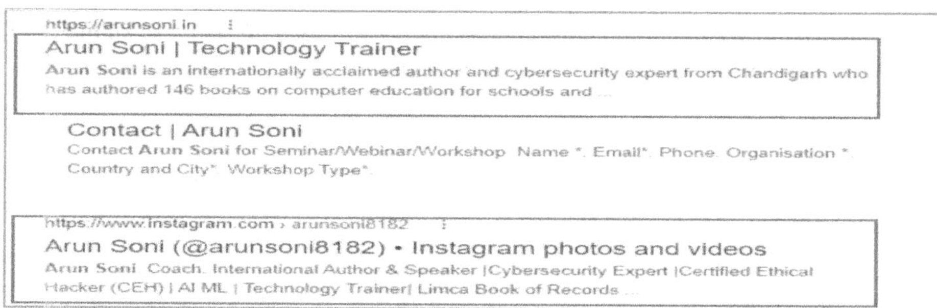

3. You will get various types of information from multiple links.

You can also search by images by visiting the link https://images.google.com/. It is called reverse image search.

WORKSHEET

Tick (✓) the correct and cross (✗) the wrong options.

a. Digital footprint and Physical footprints on sand are of the same type.

b. It would be best if you create positive digital footprints.

c. Posting a nasty comment on someone's profile is a positive digital footprint.

d. Writinga blog to review a book (let us say- How to win friends) is a negative footprint.

e. You cannot search yourself on the Google search engine by the image.

Do the following actions.

1. Search your name in the Google search engine and write down which information you find about yourself.

____

2. Search your phone number in the Google search engine and write down which information you find about yourself.

____

3. Search your profile image of a social media platform in the Google search engine and write down which information you find about yourself.

____

15 Practising Digital Hygiene

a. All about Digital Hygiene
b. Digital safety for individuals and enterprise

Digital hygiene reassures individuals to perform routine-based digital practices to minimize cyber risks. In a nutshell, Digital Hygiene refers to the cleanliness of one's digital environment. This process includes habits like learning how to choose passwords, organizing files on your laptop, adjusting the privacy settings on your social media accounts, and taking care of every connected device to increase security.

Since the COVID-19 pandemic, our interaction with the digital has reached previously unimaginable levels. As a result, identity theft, hacking, the misinformation epidemic,' data breaches, phishing, and other cyber risks have all skyrocketed. So enhanced cybersecurity has become a requirement for all users operating on digital networks.

Mitesh's mother got a new laptop for him because of the Covid-19 the school, shifted to online classes. He was excited as it was the latest laptop in the market. It was the first time he was operating it, the first time in the presence of his mother.

Mitesh, I am afraid they are not maintaining Digital hygiene. Sooner or later, they will face a lot of malware problems, crashing of software and might get fined by companies whose pirated software they are using. We must perform routine-based digital practices to minimize cyber risks.
Digital Hygiene !? What is that, mom?
Digital hygiene is a critical first line of defence against emerging digital threats such as malicious emails, social engineering, phishing, online harassment, hacking accounts and devices, attempting to steal private data, and worse. You can see that we already have taken the first step towards it by installing all genuine software and a trustworthy antivirus.
Mom, I am curious. Tell me more about it. I do not want to remain safe in cyberspace.

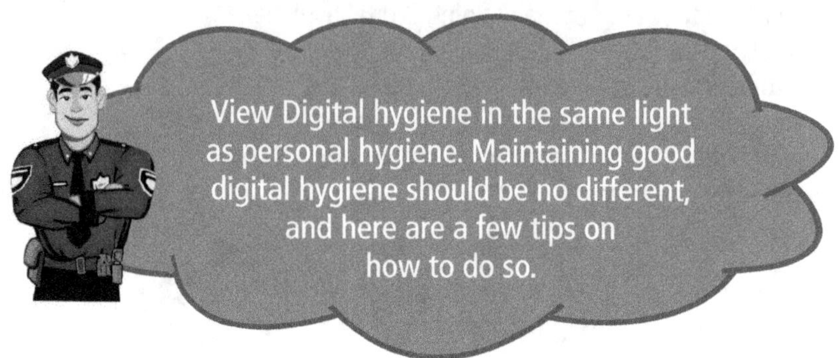

How to practice digital safety and security

Following are some steps you can take to practice digital safety and maintain digital hygiene. These apply to an individual as well as an enterprise.

- Companies update their software and applications regularly to address security issues. Ensure you update your operating system software and other applications as soon as updates become available. Your OS, browser, firewall and antivirus should always get automatically updated as soon as updates arrive.

- A strong password can make a significant difference in preventing cyberattacks. A password is considered "strong" if at least ten characters long and contains a mix of letters, numbers, and symbols. Better use a passphrase instead of a password. All your accounts should have a unique password.

- While social media platforms can be enjoyable, you should be aware that they broadcast a wealth of information about you. And also about your colleagues and your organization to anyone, including malicious actors. Limit the publicly available information about you online, especially to strangers.

- Learn about encryption. Encryption makes things unreadable for prying eyes. Learn about end-to-end encryption, which makes communication fully secure. Use VPNs for securing your data and browsing a private experience.

- Encrypt any backups of all crucial files in external hard drives and cloud services. Many free software and utilities are built within an operating system to encrypt the files.

- Change the default search engine to a privacy-oriented website such as DuckDuckGo, Brave and Opera. Regularly clear your cache and history.

- Change the name of your Wi-Fi network to something less recognizable.

- Your router and personal smart devices connected to your home internet should have their default passwords changed.

- Install security browser extensions on all of your browsers, regardless of which one you are using. *HTTPS Everywhere, Privacy Badger, Netcraft* and *NoScript* contribute to internet browsing safety (Search for their uses on the Internet).

- Regularly review and delete any browser extensions that you don't often use.

- Do not attempt to click on any suspicious links. If in doubt, use www.virustotal.com to verify the link before clicking.

- Do not be rude to anyone or make abusive or indecent comments to any post.

- Data breaches, hacking of businesses, and the theft of sensitive information are becoming increasingly common. As a business, it is critical to identify areas of vulnerability. Your organization must educate its employees about digital hygiene.

- When onboarding new employees, you can provide digital hygiene and cybersecurity training. This way, you can raise immediate awareness among your employees and encourage them to improve.

- Encourage your employees to share their mistakes to avoid a situation where someone attempts to conceal their error and worsens an already dangerous situation.

PRACTICE Time

To install Netcraft extension in your chrome browser. (Netcraft chrome extension provides complete website information and phishing protection while browsing the web).

1. In the Google Search Engine, search for **Netcraft Extension for Chrome**. Click on the first link which appears in the search.

2. The Chrome Web Store web page opens and will show the Netcraft Extension option to add to your browser. Click on the **Add to Chrome**.

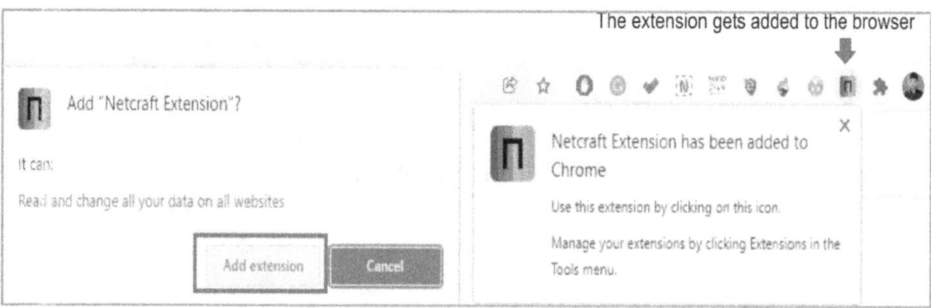

3. Click on **Add Extension** to add the extension to your browser. The extension will get added to the browser.

WORKSHEET

1 **Tick (✓) the correct answers.**

a. Which one of these browsers provides you with the maximum privacy?

1. Edge
2. Chrome
3. Firefox
4. DuckDuckGo

b. It is a browser extension that stops advertisers and other third-party trackers from secretly tracking your online activities?

1. HTTPS Everywhere
2. Privacy Badger
3. Netcraft
4. NoScript

2 **Write down three features of each browser that you think are noteworthy.**

S.No.	DuckDuckGo	Brave	Opera	Firefox
1				
2				
3				

Reporting a Cyber Crime

You should report a cybercrime at the earliest so that the Cyber cell can take immediate action against the culprit. Since Cybercrime is borderless and electronic, it can spread much faster than you realize, put you in a financial crisis and damage your reputation.

Almost every state or country has a dedicated website and helpline number to report Cybercrime. You can report a cybercrime through the relevant options given on the portal. Do not forget to attach the 'digital' evidence along with the complaint.

Digital evidence could be a screenshot of the message sent by the harasser or the fake social media id. It can be anything that proves that you are a victim of any Cybercrime.

Hey!

I am from India. Where do I complain about Cybercrime?

Visit www.cybercrime.gov.in. There you can report the incident. You will also get the complaint number to follow the complaint. You can also approach the nearest police station to file the complaint. The national helpline no. to report Cybercrime is 1930.

I am from the UK. Where should I file the complaint?

You report at https://www.ic3.gov/

Hey!

There are so many countries. Why don't you check http://www.ccmostwanted.com/report-cybercrime-worldwide/ to know about websites for most countries where you can file complaints.

GLOSSARY

A

Antivirus

Antivirus software, often known as anti-malware software, was first introduced a few years ago to protect computers from viruses and other simple threats. Antivirus software now protects users from more sophisticated online threats (malware in the broad sense) such as ransomware, rootkits, trojans, malware, phishing attempts, and botnets.

Attack Vector

It is a specific method used by a hacker to accomplish his malicious goal.

APT (Advanced Persistent Threat)

It is a security breach that allows an attacker to obtain access to or control a system over an extended time without the system's owner being aware of it. An APT frequently uses several of the undisclosed flaws or zero-day assaults, allowing the attacker to keep access to the target even when some attack vectors are blocked.

Authentication

A username and password are typically used in an individual's authentication (or identification). This method is utilized to grant access to an online site or resource to the appropriate person by validating identification.

B

Backup

A backup is a full copy of your data, system files, or other system resources you want to safeguard. This precaution is required in the event of any unforeseeable incident such as a system crash or deletion/ loss of files. In some situations, the system or those files become contaminated, and you must recover them. Or when a ransomware infection prevents access to the system.

Botnet

A botnet is a network of infected computers that collaborate to carry out malicious acts, such as spam campaigns or distributed denial-of-service assaults.

Bug

A bug is an error in software coding or the design or manufacturing of hardware. A bug is a weakness or vulnerability in a system that attackers can exploit as a point of compromise.

Buffer Overflow

When software or application tries to store too much data in a temporary storage space (a buffer), the extra data overflows into other portions of the computer's memory. It is called a buffer overflow. Hackers take advantage of this, and these types of attacks might result in the execution of unwanted code or system crashes.

C

Cookie

When you visit a website, a cookie is a tiny text file that is stored on your computer. This cookie enables the website to store your preferences and keep track of your visit details. These cookies were created to aid in the speeding up of the website the next time you visit that place. At the same time, advertisers benefit from them because they can tailor adverts to your preferences based on your surfing history.

Code Injection

Online attackers frequently employ the code injection technique to alter the course of a computer program's execution. Online fraudsters utilize this strategy to spread harmful software by injecting malicious code into genuine websites.

Command & Control Centre

A command and control centre (C&C) is a network server that is in charge of a huge network of infected computers. Hackers utilize the malicious server to send and receive instructions from and to affected systems. Hackers can use this type of network to launch distributed denial-of-service attacks by telling all computers to do the same thing.

Cryptography

The study of secure communications techniques that allow only the sender and intended recipient of a message to read its contents is known as cryptography. It is closely linked to encryption, which scrambles plain text into ciphertext and then back again when it's received.

D

Data Integrity
Data integrity refers to information that hasn't been tampered with or changed by an unauthorized party. Information quality in a database or other online place is referred to as this phrase.

Data Breach
A data breach occurs when sensitive information is disclosed, accessed confidential information is destroyed, or abusive use of a private IT environment. Internal data is typically made accessible to external bodies without consent due to a data breach.

Denial Of Service (DoS) attack
This kind of cyber attack is designed to prevent ordinary people from accessing a website. In this example, a cybercriminal can prohibit genuine users from accessing a website by relying on its network resources and flooding it with information requests.

Drive-by download attack
It is a kind of web-based attack that arises due to simply accessing a malicious or affected website. A drive-by download is performed by utilizing a Web browser's usual functionality to execute code, most commonly JavaScript, with little to no security limitations. A drive-by download can install tracking tools, remote access backdoors, botnet agents, keystroke loggers, and other malicious applications.

Digital Signature
A digital signature is a method of encrypting and validating a communication, software, or digital document's integrity. A hacker will find it difficult to reproduce a digital signature, which is why it is vital in information security.

E

Exploit
An exploit is a piece of software, a chunk of data, or a series of commands that exploits a software defect, a flaw, or a vulnerability to access a user's system with nefarious intent.

Eavesdropping Attack
Network eavesdropping, also known as network sniffing, is a type of attack

that seeks to intercept data sent over a network by other computers. The goal is to obtain sensitive information such as passwords, session tokens, or any other type of confidential data.

Encryption
Encryption is the process of transforming plaintext information (or a message) into a difficult-to-read form called ciphertext using an encryption algorithm.

End-to-end encryption
End-to-end encryption (E2EE) is a secure communication technology that prevents third parties from gaining access to data as it moves from one end system or device to another. E2EE additionally protects encrypted messages against tampering.

F

Firewall
A firewall is a software or hardware-based network security device that prevents unwanted access to public or private networks. Its goal is to use a set of rules to govern incoming and outgoing communication.

Forensic specialist
A forensic specialist in IT security is a person who examines and analyses web traffic and data transfer in order to come to a conclusion based on the gathered facts.

G

Greyhat hackers
Greyhat hackers operate ambiguously than blackhat and whitehat hackers. They may, for example, utilize illicit tactics to discover a vulnerability before disclosing it to the targeted firm. And then sell the information to a company in exchange for a fee.

H

Hacker
A hacker is someone who succeeds to obtain unauthorized access to a computer system with the intent of causing harm. However, keep in mind that

there are two types of hackers: whitehat hackers who conduct penetration testing and report their findings to aid in developing more secure systems and software, and blackhat hackers who employ their expertise for evil purposes.

Hacktivism

Hacktivism is the act of protesting against or fighting for political and social goals using hacking tactics. Anonymous is one of the most well-known hacktivist groups in the world.

Hash

A hash is an algorithm for transforming a vast amount of data into an encrypted output of a fixed length that can be compared without having to convert it to plaintext. In bitcoin, a hash is an essential aspect of blockchain administration.

Honeypot

A honeypot is a network-attached system that serves as a decoy to attract cyber attackers and detect, divert, and investigate hacking attempts to gain unauthorized access to information systems. The purpose of a honeypot is to portray itself on the Internet as a prospective target for attackers (typically a server or other high-value asset). Moreover, it collects data, analyses the attacker's methodology, and warns defenders of unwanted attempts to access the honeypot.

I

Identity Theft

Identity theft is the act of taking someone's personal identity information and utilizing it to impersonate that person online. Hackers can use a person's name, photographs, documents, social security/Aadhar card number, and other personal information to gain a financial advantage at their expense (by acquiring credit or blackmailing) or harm the person's reputation, among other things.

Information Security

The techniques, methods, measures, and actions used to prevent unauthorized access, use, disclosure, interruption, alteration, or destruction of data and information systems. Its goal is to secure the confidentiality, integrity, and availability of the data and information systems.

Integrity

This is one of the fundamental concepts of cyber security. It refers to the need to guarantee that information has not been tampered with (either intentionally or inadvertently) and that data is correct and complete.

Intellectual Property

This refers to creative, technological, or industrial information, thoughts, ideas, or knowledge that demonstrate who owns them, either in tangible form or representation.

IP Spoofing

Cyber fraudsters utilize this technique to provide a false IP address that appears to be valid. This aids the attacker in gaining an unfair edge and deceiving the user or a cyber security solution.

Intrusion Prevention Systems (IPS)

It is a security tool that tries to detect attempts to breach a target's security and then prevents the attack from succeeding. Because it tries to respond to potential attacks proactively, an IPS is considered a more active security instrument. In the event of a cyber attack, IP addresses can be blocked, services can be turned off, ports can be blocked, and sessions can be disconnected, and administrators can be notified.

J

Javascript

It is a programming language for creating and controlling website content, allowing you to design the behaviour of web pages to do a specific task.

Jailbreaking

To remove an operating system's constraints from a device running that operating system, particularly iOS. The act of breaking into jail is a sort of privilege escalation. Because users frequently jailbreak their own devices, the legality of jailbreaking is determined by end-user licence agreements and applicable legislation.

JBOH (JavaScript-Binding-Over-HTTP)

An Android-specific mobile device attack that allows an attacker to start the execution of malicious scripts on a compromised device. A JBOH attack is frequently carried out or helped by compromised or malicious apps.

K

Keylogger
Cybercriminals can employ malicious software to capture keystrokes on a user's keyboard without the victim's knowledge through keylogging. Cybercriminals can gather information such as passwords, usernames, PINs, and other sensitive information this way.

Kernel
It is the core of a computer's operating system that houses the computer's most essential functions.

L

Least Privilege
The idea of least privilege states that users or apps should have the fewest permissions essential to execute their intended job.

Logic bomb
A logic bomb is a piece of code that is placed into a system with the intent of triggering a malicious programme. Logic bombs are common in viruses and worms, and they execute a certain payload at a pre-determined time or when a certain condition is satisfied.

M

Malware
This is a shorter version of "malicious software". It serves as an umbrella term for software with malicious purposes. This malicious software can disrupt regular computer operations, collect sensitive data, gain unauthorized access to computer systems, display unwanted advertising, and more.

Man-in-the-middle Attack (MitM)
Cybercriminals can use this technique to alter the victim's web traffic and place themselves between the victim and a web-based service the victim is attempting to access. At that moment, the attacker can either collect or alter the information being broadcast over the Internet.

Metadata
Seemingly harmless impersonal data, like how many times a user clicked or

refreshed the page when visiting a website or the date and time of a clicked photograph through a smartphone/digital camera.

Muti-Factor Authentication(MFA)
To achieve MFA, this sort of authentication employs two or more factors. These factors can include something the user knows (a password or a PIN). Another factor can be that the user has - an SMS with a code or a code generator on the phone/tablet and biometric authentication methods, such as fingerprints or retina scans.

N

Netiquette
Netiquette (short for "network etiquette") is a set of social norms to make online interactions constructive, reasonable, and beneficial.

Network Sniffing
It is a technique that uses a software program to monitor and analyze network traffic. It is used legitimately to detect problems and keep an efficient data flow. But it can also be used maliciously to harvest data transmitted over a network.

O

Outside Threat
An unauthorized individual outside the company's security perimeter can harm an information system by destroying it, altering or stealing data from it, releasing it to unauthorized recipients, and triggering an attack vector like denial of service.

P

Patch
A patch is a little software update that manufacturers deploy to fix or improve a program. A patch can address security flaws or other defects and improve the software's functionality, usability, and performance.

Penetration Testing
This is a network or computer system attack that aims to find security flaws that can be exploited to obtain unauthorized access to the network's/features

system's and data. Penetration testing is a method of assisting businesses in better defending themselves against cyber-attacks.

Phishing

It is the practice of acquiring user information through deceptive communications sent directly to individuals. This is commonly accomplished through emails that appear to be from a reputable source but actually transmit the target's information to the hacker's source.

Payload

In cyber-security, the payload is the component of malware software that performs a destructive activity. Activities might result in data loss, theft of confidential information, and damage to computer-based systems or processes.

Q

Quick Response Code Login jacking (QRLJacking) is a simple but dangerous attack vector that affects all applications that use the "Login with QR code" function as a secure way to enter into accounts. In a nutshell, it's all about persuading the victim to scan the attacker's QR code.

R

Ransomware

Ransomware is a sort of malware (malicious software) that encrypts all of the data on a computer or mobile device and prevents the data owner from accessing it. After the infection, the victim receives a message stating that a particular amount of money (typically in Bitcoins) must be paid in order to obtain the decryption key.

Reverse Engineering

It is a common strategy used by cyber security researchers that regularly dissect malware to examine it. This allows them to understand better and watch how the malware operates and develop security solutions to protect consumers from that sort of malware and its techniques.

Risk Management

This is how a company manages its cyber security risks to reduce their potential impact and take the necessary precautions to avert cyber assaults.

S

Scareware

This sort of malware (also known as rogueware) uses social engineering to scare and baffle victims by instilling fear, anxiety, and time constraints. Malicious actors, for example, frequently try to convince customers that their machine is infected with a virus. And that the only way to remove it is to pay for, download, and install a false antivirus, which, of course, is the malware itself.

Sensitive Information

Sensitive data is private information to a specific group of users who can see, access, and utilize it. This type of information is kept confidential for various reasons, including legal and ethical concerns.

Signature

A signature is an identifiable, distinguishing pattern linked with a type of malware to gain unauthorized access to a system. Traditional antivirus software, for example, may detect, block, and remove malware based on its signature.

Spear Phishing

Spear phishing is a type of cyber assault that uses a highly targeted and personalized message to gather sensitive information from a victim. This message is frequently given to individuals or businesses, and it is mighty due to its meticulous planning.

Secure Sockets Layer (SSL)

Secure Sockets Layer, or SSL, is an encryption method for ensuring the security of data transferred and received from a user to a specified website and back. Encrypting this data transfer ensures that no one can eavesdrop on it and obtain access to sensitive information, such as credit card numbers, in the case of online purchasing.

T

Threat

Any situation or occurrence that has the potential to impair an information system by allowing unauthorized access, destruction, disclosure, data alteration, and/or denial of service.

Threat Hunting

Threat hunting is the proactive use of manual or machine-based tactics by a skilled cybersecurity analyst to uncover security incidents or threats that existing automated detection systems like firewall or IDS/IPS have missed.

Token

A token is a physical, electronic device used to verify a user's identification in the field of security. Tokens are commonly used as part of two-factor or multi-factor authentication systems. Tokens can be found in the form of a key, a USB, an ID card, or a smart card and can be used to substitute passwords in some instances.

U

URL Injection

When a hacker creates/injects new pages on an existing website, this is known as URL injection. These pages frequently contain code that directs viewers to other websites or engages the company in attacks on other websites. Software flaws, insecure directories, and plug-ins can all be used to implant malware.

V

VPN

A VPN, or virtual private network, is an encrypted link between a device and a network/document over the Internet. Sensitive data is safely delivered thanks to the encrypted connection. It also hides your online identity by changing your IP Address.

Vishing

Vishing (short for Voice over IP phishing) is a form of phishing performed over the telephone or voice over IP (VoIP) technology, such as Skype. Unsuspecting victims are duped into revealing sensitive or personal information via telephone calls, VoIP calls or even voice mail.

Vulnerability

A vulnerability is a flaw in computer security that allows cyber attackers to damage the system data. Vulnerabilities must be addressed as soon as they are identified before a cybercriminal exploits them.

W

Wardriving

Wardriving is when a person in a moving vehicle uses a portable computer, smartphone, or personal digital assistant to look for wi-fi wireless networks.

Wiretapping

Wiretapping is the process of continuously monitoring and recording data travelling between two points in a communication system.

Whaling

Whaling is a highly-targeted form of spear phishing aimed at senior executives within an organization.

Y

The year 2000 bug, sometimes known as the millennium bug, is abbreviated as Y2k. Bob Bemer first released the Y2k warning in 1971, detailing the problems with computers that use a two-digit year date stamp.

Z

zero-day attack

A zero-day (or zero-hour or day zero) attack is a cyber-threat that tries to exploit computer application vulnerabilities that the software developer is unaware of. Zero-day exploits are pieces of code that can take advantage of a security flaw to launch an attack.

Zombie

A zombie computer is an internet-connected computer that has been hacked, infected with a computer virus, or infected with a trojan horse. In most cases, a compromised system is just one of many in a botnet that is used to carry out destructive actions under remote control.